Dreams of the Moon

a collection of short fiction

Lorina Stephens

FIVE RIVERS PUBLISHING
FIVERIVERSPUBLISHING.COM

Published by Five Rivers Publishing, 704 Queen Street, P.O. Box 293, Neustadt, ON N0G 2M0, Canada.

fiveriverspublishing.com

interior design and layout by Lorina Stephens.

Titles set in Trinigan FG, an Art Nouveau typeface well-known via advertising and the silver screen. .

Text set in Chaparral Pro, designed by Carol Twombly for Adobe.

Published in Canada

Library and Archives Canada Cataloguing in Publication

Title: Dreams of the moon : a collection of short fiction / Lorina Stephens.

Names: Stephens, Lorina, 1955- author.

Identifiers: Canadiana 20210153776 | ISBN 9781988274690 (softcover)

Classification: LCC PS8587.T4654 D74 2021 | DDC C813/.54—dc23) for Gary, as always

Contents

Foreword

The last collection of short stories I published was in 2008. It's an eclectic mix which I entitled *And the Angels Sang,* named for the lead story. To my delight, it's met with quite a bit of positive reaction from both readers and reviewers.

In the ensuing years, I've crafted a number of other short stories in between operating a publishing house and all the demands of being an administrator in our other business, one which pays the bills. A lot has happened during that time: our son married his life-buddy, three major surgeries, a failed attempt at elder care, renovating this old stone house which was built c1847, and as I write this, into the second year of a global pandemic.

And somewhere in all that still writing, still exploring ideas and what-ifs. I do have to admit a reluctance to writing short fiction. The literary form seems so restrictive to me, perhaps more having to do with the fact I have too much to say and want to make an epic out of everything. But short story writing is good discipline.

Having said that, I'm giving you 10 short works of fiction in this collection, spanning the boundaries of science fiction, speculative fiction, fantasy, magic realism and absurd fantastica. Apparently,

I don't much like writing in just one genre, either. Creative fences drive me batshit crazy, although I do very much appreciate fences around this sanctuary we are privileged to call home. But there is a theme to this collection, a common thread I think you will find through all the stories. What it is, I will leave up to you to decipher, and thus we will have a silent communication.

I've arranged the stories in some loose graduation of dark to light, and again have chosen to use the lead story as the title for the collection. But the title *Dreams of the Moon* is more, because as a child, and then an adolescent, I firmly believed if I arranged myself just so in the bed, so that when the moon shone in my window, something wonderful would happen. It never did. But I still felt compelled to answer the call of that pale, eerie light.

And then there were all the moonlight walks in the deep of the night which took place well into adulthood. Wonderful moments. Moments I remember with clarity and wonder, whether moonlight so bright on a winter's night that the trees by the river cast indigo shadows across the snow, or a brace of geese rising up and across that silver face. And as with all things, there is the dark side of the moon: a sleepless night fraught with sorrow and a desperate attempt to rescue someone I dearly loved.

All of these moments influence and underscore what I write. It's there in these 10 stories. Darkness and light. Wonder and sorrow. The ambiguity, sometimes, of reflected light. Dreams of the Moon.

Dreams of the Moon

First published in Stories of the Deluge, Allen Taylor, ed.

In the darkness that follows disaster, he hears the river. It sounds like the rush of beating wings, pulling the host of Elohim into conflict, and for some, into escape. He is unsure who has followed, or who has betrayed them. Michael? Raphael? Whom among the Iyrin hadn't wanted to teach those beautiful mortals?

He gropes the air before him, feels nothing, moves toward the sound of the river, finds a rough texture under his fingers – bark, it's still here – and hands himself down to sit beneath the tree. There is pain. This is something new to him, a sinister sensation in the darkness, he who has lived his life in the chiaroscuro of light. Sariel, whose name was written on shields, whose name was an invocation of death from the Third Tower and he, the Bringer of Death. The Captain Sariel now blind, unable to fly, waiting here at the edge of the river and the fourth paradise for what he's unsure and wishing for death.

He thinks he might laugh for the absurdity of it. Too much to think about. Too much has happened. He eases further down in darkness to fragrant myrtle, dew on his arm, pain in one wing where he knows it's broken, pain where his eyes once saw the phases of the moon. He lets the darkness and the rush of the river become an anodyne for his senses.

That is the problem, isn't it? That the senses can overtake you, that one of the chosen ten captains of tens can succumb to beauty and feel the need to nurture it, embrace it, teach it all the wonders of the moon. It is a problem when one of the Iyrin challenges authority. It is disaster when it is many. He remembers evacuating Adam and Eve to the Cave of Treasures, the air filled with thousands of wings, an exodus of The Chosen, and exile for the beloved of the Iyrin. The Chosen and the Nephilim, the children the Iyrin gave to them. His beloved. His child. Now lost to him.

He listens to the river. There is only one way to cross it now. Impossible to fly with this broken wing and sightless eyes.

"Sariel," he hears, and stirs, unsure if he's imagining this through the miasma of his pain. He wishes he could see. He wishes he could know the minds of others as he once had.

"Shamsiel?" he asks. His voice sounds hoarse to him, a rattle in the darkness.

"No," the voice answers. "Shamsiel is fallen."

Fallen. Then Eden has fallen, for Shamsiel and that host were to defend Eden. All is lost. "Are they safe? The Chosen, the Nephilim?" Is she safe? Is the child?

"Yes. We're all safe."

And doomed to exist on Mount Hermon in the Cave of Treasures, they and their Nephilim. "And the other Iyrin with us?"

"All fallen. You are the last."

With that realization Sariel weeps. He cannot help it. So much has been lost. So much beauty. Down into darkness. The City of Light is no longer theirs, nor is the world they'd hoped to make with The Chosen and the children they would rear together.

He feels lips on his eyes, hears the voice of his rescuer, sibilant sounds in the darkness. There are words meant to comfort, words meant to soothe, and Sariel sinks into the other's arms, letting grief wash over him. It is the woman he's taken as mate he now knows. Her hands touch his face, the wounds of his eyes. He can feel her trembling, or is that him?

"I know, I know," she says, and there is rocking, something the Iyrin learned from mortal humans, an expression of a need for comfort. "Only a little more pain now. And it will all be done."

But a little more pain explodes into suffocating terror. He screams. And then again as the terror repeats. The darkness is filled with the sound of it, the smell of it. With one hand he reaches out toward her, finds an arm, a hand. The hilt of his own fiery sword has been used to sever wings, and now he is truly afraid because her voice still croons, and she still rocks him.

"Why?" he manages to gasp.

"To bind you. To disguise you against the hunt that has come. All the others have been cast forever into darkness, and I would have you live, and live with me. Be mortal. Die."

Sariel, the Prince of Death to die himself.

He sinks into oblivion, unable to bear the pain. When again he rises he is still in darkness, still rocking, only now there is music, a voice in melancholy song. In another moment of panic realizes he's on a boat.

He calls out. He hears her voice.

"You're awake," she says

"Where are you taking me?" He knows, but there is always hope. He's learned this from his sojourn in Eden.

"To the others."

"And so we are all outcasts?"

"All. And bound."

"Is this death?"

"Very like, I suppose."

She dissembles, he knows. "How?" He can hear no answer, and bound in darkness he cannot see any gesture that might illuminate the question. It is then he confronts the fact of mortality, of what it was to be Iyrin. He has heard for the dead there is cessation of pain. It is what he believed being the Prince of Death. So many lives he has translated with the power of his sword. But, for the Iyrin there would be everlasting knowledge of what they've lost and will never again see, or know, cast out as others are. She has given him a choice, now, to live or to die.

And so Sariel, father of one of the Nephilim, mate of a human woman, once favoured among the Iyrin, master of the phases of the moon, does what he is doomed to do: he seizes that fiery sword, pushes himself out of the boat and smites himself. He sinks down into the frigid water, dreaming of beauty. Dreaming of death.

At Union

First published in Postcripts to Darkness 5

It's late, or early, depending on your perspective, but he doesn't care and so he walks across the main gallery of Union Station: just like anyone else catching a train, leaving a train, meeting a train, the heels of his shoes creaking on marble. The sound echoes with other footsteps, creates a susurration that laps at these Edwardian vaults. Union never sleeps. Some people who arrive at Union never sleep.

"For the right price you can meet a train from anywhere," she'd said; the bag-lady who had heaved herself down to the stool beside him. He'd been drinking Tim Horton's coffee and staunching a haemorrhaging heart.

He'd looked at her, the missing teeth, the red paisley of her kerchief tied under the crepe of her chin. Her breath had been foul, her eyes feral-bright.

"What makes you think I'm looking for a train?"

"Everyone at Union is looking for a train." She'd sipped her coffee, pulled his honey-glazed across the laminate counter and ate the pastry. "Everyone at Union is on their way to a destination, an assignation, a breath of what might or could be." She'd dabbed at her mouth with a paper serviette. "Pay the gatekeeper, you see Kathy."

Remembering, he feels a hard thump where his heart should be. He places a nitroglycerin tablet under his tongue, feels the familiar tingling in his mouth. He's through the entrance to the trains, steps onto the escalator to take him down into the metro of Union, Go trains, Via Rail trains, pays his fare for the TTC trains and in his impatience he weaves around other people, his pace increasing until he reaches the end of the platform, and there he walks, briskly now, toward a guitarist, bald and tattooed like a dispossessed Maori, picking blues.

Two weeks since that chance encounter with a homeless woman. Two weeks to think about the ridiculousness of what she'd said. What could he lose by investigating? What would he lose by not?

It's dim here, not like the golden glory of the main entrance, as though Union decays from the bowels. Or is forgotten.

How fitting, then, the archway he seeks is a darker tunnel in the dimness of the platform, and that the guitarist's raw riff hangs like smoke.

As he's walking, he plunges his hand into the pocket of his navy trousers, feels for significant coin and tosses a couple of twoonies into the guitarist's open case. He keeps walking, heart hammering.

At his back he hears, "Where you goin' ain't no peace, bro."

But the gatekeeper is paid. The forms have been met. He has done as instructed, and keeps walking into the corridor. He thinks this is like a birth canal, but instead of to life, he walks to death. And his daughter. She will be here. He's arranged it with that payment to the gatekeeper. Bought the bag-lady's story that Toronto's rails could carry the souls of those you've loved and lost if you knew where to ask, where to look, what to pay. There is always a cost, whether monetary or otherwise didn't matter now. She would be here.

She will be here.

As he steps out of the arched corridor he confronts a scene out of the murk of dreams. There are people like him populating the concrete platform, and among them others dressed in grey, like modern Franciscans, or cucullati: grey suits, white shirts; one guide for each person waiting for the train. It's all very monochrome. It's all very orderly. He wasn't sure what he'd been expecting, perhaps some d'anse macabre tableau, but certainly not this hushed, colourless civility.

For a moment he hesitates where corridor meets platform, watching, unsure, speculating on the possibility of his madness for believing he could once more see his girl, speak with her, share a moment of stolen time. He thinks, not for the first time, children are not supposed to die before their parents, before their fathers; she wasn't supposed to die before him.

She'd fought so hard to stay alive. Kathy always fought. Killer Kathy. His girl.

Fucking leukemia.

A young man detaches from the amorphous grey and stands before him.

"You're Robert Fowler," the young man says, not a question, gaze direct, face like polished marble. Vaguely, Robert wonders if this fellow ever needs to shave.

He dips his head in a nod.

The young man gestures to the milling crowd. "This way. The train's due any moment."

"You have a name?" He wants a name. There have been two too many people without names involved in this. A name will help him navigate.

"Malek," the fellow answers. Malek gestures again. "Come."

Robert feels the fellow's hand on his elbow, a gentle but insistent pressure, and desperate he allows himself to be guided into the crowd.

"You understand the restrictions?" Malek says.

Robert nods. "We visit here. We're not to leave the platform. Twenty minutes until the next train which takes her away. Twenty-four hours before I can see her again."

"Good." Malek checks his watch. "Don't forget you are not to touch her."

He opens his mouth to ask why, but hears the rattle and screech of a train slowing for the station, and in a moment the sound becomes a roar, and the flinty smell of steel on steel fills the air, the scream of brakes, hiss of doors sliding open and away. And in the doorways of the trains stand passengers pale of face, sombre, their fear a palpable thing that shivers over his arms and thuds in his heart.

Malek, like his fellow grey-friars, steps forward through the crowd, each escort seeking out their charge and returning to the waiting wives and husbands, daughters and sons, mothers. And fathers.

He sees Kathy. She looks as grey as Malek's suit, the pallor she wore lying there in that hospital bed with her bone marrow neuked and the stem-cell transplant failing to reboot her system. Twenty-eight and no way to die. His face is wet with tears and he hears himself gasping for air.

"Kathy," he whispers. He's about to say, How are you? and realizes how ridiculous that is. What do you say to your dead daughter?

"Dad," she says and although there are no tears on her face he hears the catch in her throat. She looks scared, he thinks, and wants to pull her to his side, drape his arm around her shoulders and squeeze. Maybe he'd been wrong? Maybe you didn't screw with the forces of nature?

"C'mon," he says, and gestures toward the archway where there are fewer people and the light is dimmer. "We can talk over there."

Malek precedes them, places himself like a barrier in front of the corridor. Robert tries to ignore him, walking to the wall, glancing over his shoulder to make sure Kathy follows. She does, but it's clear she's uncomfortable. When at last they're cross-legged on the ground – where else would you find a man in a navy business suit sitting on the floor? – he asks her if she needs anything.

She looks at him, perplexed. "What would I need?"

"I don't know."

Her attention slides away again, flicking from person to person, the walls, the floor, the rails where the trains run every twenty minutes.

"I've missed you," he says. "Every day."

"I know," she says. And is silent once more.

The pain in his chest increases. Suddenly he doesn't know how to navigate. There are no familiar landmarks. His easy banter with his living daughter died on her hospital bed. What do you say to your dead daughter? What could he possibly give her?

So he asks the difficult question. "What's it like?"

She looks at him.

"Being dead."

"It's...." She looks away and down. The pallid skin of her brow creases. He wants to touch that and smooth it away, give her some comfort. She looks back up at him with eyes that are dark like polished onyx, reflecting everything, revealing nothing. It's a shock to him. Kathy's eyes had been a remarkable hazel, olive green round the rims, nut brown near the iris, filled with gold flecks so that as a child she'd reminded him of some stolen foundling. He remembered thinking how lucky he was to have been entrusted to raise this creature, to watch her grow.

And then watch her die. She had been so fearless where he had not.

"What?" he prompts, feeling his way. "It's what?"

She shrugs and looks down. "It's nothing."

"You're not aware of anything?"

"No."

"Not even on the train?"

"The train? Oh, yes, the train. Yes. It's like waking up after being drugged. It's...."

"Hard?"

"Yes." She looks back up at him, a moment of anger like flash-fire across her face then gone, smoothed back into a placid sheet. "Why am I here?"

"Because I missed you."

"It's not natural. The dead should be left dead."

"Kathy...."

"It's time," Malek says, and instantly Robert is angry. The hell with rules. The hell with them all. This is his daughter, and he'd be damned –

Malek rises and gestures to Kathy, who also rises. They turn toward the platform. Robert can hear the train rumbling, like a monstrous worm in this subterranean mausoleum.

"I'll be back," Robert says as Kathy retreats.

"Then I will be too."

The train stops. The doors open. The grey-friars escort their charges aboard and the train lurches forward and away.

Robert sinks back to the floor, draws his knees up, wraps his arms around them and weeps.

* * *

He spends the next two weeks travelling to Union in the middle of the night, waiting for the dead train. He brings Kathy a double-double one time, only to drink it himself when she says that the dead don't drink. Their conversation remains stilted. He longs to embrace her. He's desperate to find a way to make her less nervous, draw her out, see her quicksilver smile and know she's okay. That she is okay. But how can she be okay when she's dead and a walking corpse drawn here because of some insane pact he's made with a bag-lady witch and a blues-picking guitarist?

One night, after she's gone again, he pauses and asks Malek about what's happening here, about the improbable reality that he's visiting with his daughter.

"They come because they've been summoned," Malek answers.

"So this has nothing to do with their will?"

"They have no will. They're dead."

"Then this is an abomination."

"It would be an abomination if you forced them to remain."

Robert walks away thinking about that, wondering how wanting to live could be wrong.

He thinks maybe he should ask his ex-wife about that. Call her. Break the silence of the years. But then no. How to explain this thing?

That night, with Malek guarding the corridor, and Kathy sitting with him on the floor, Robert asks her, "Do you want to come home with me?"

Malek straightens. Robert feels the grey-friar's tension.

"Why?" she asks.

"So you wouldn't have to go back to being dead."

"But that's what I am."

"Not when you're with me."

"Robert," Malek says. He can hear the warning in the grey-friar's voice.

"Stay out of this."

"It's my job to stay in this."

"I don't know," Kathy answers and hangs her head.

The train screeches in. Kathy rises, turns with Malek. Not even a goodbye. This time Robert leaves before the train pulls away, unable to watch, unable to accept this twilight world in which he now lives. He escapes through the corridor, past the blues-picking gatekeeper, up escalators and across platforms, through the train entrance and back out to the main gallery of Union where he thumps down on a bench and stares out at nothing.

He's exhausted. For weeks now he's kept up this small hours vigil, snatching sleep in shifts and fits. There's work to be done, calls to return, email to which to respond. He shivers, scrubs his fingers over his eyes. He needs a coffee before returning home.

The bag-lady with the red paisley scarf slides onto the bench beside him, offers him that coffee he wants. He looks up at her, down at the brown paper mug, at the yellow arrow that notifies the customer of a potential prize under the rim.

He digs into his pocket, comes up with two twoonies and a loonie, and folds the woman's fingers over the coins.

"Thanks," he says. He drinks down the coffee. It's rich, sweet flavour scalds his mouth and he doesn't care, lets it spill down his throat. He thinks it would be better with an Islay chaser. A whole forty ounces of Islay chaser.

"Life work out as you expected?" she says.

He lets go of a strangled laugh. She pats his knee, gestures to the empty brown paper cup. "You forgot to roll up the rim."

* * *

This time the plan is different. He has a Get-Out-of-Jail-Free card. As usual, he enters Union, makes his way through the train entrance, down the escalator, pays his fare, weaves through crowds and levels, tosses coins at the guitarist gatekeeper and is attended by Malek. He fingers the ragged square of card in his pocket, a winning coupon torn from a brown paper coffee cup. No free donut, free coffee, prize of a new car on that voucher.

As the train rumbles into the station he pulls out the torn bit of card, proffers it to Malek who stands there staring at it. Robert senses the grey-friar's anger, even his outrage, but as though facing an irresistible force Malek snatches the bit of card out of Robert's fingers. He looks up and directly at Robert.

"Remember that I did warn you. And that it wasn't because I didn't care."

Malek turns away toward the train, escorts Kathy to him and then exits into the corridor, beyond the guitarist, beyond any influence.

The first thing Robert does is fold his girl into his arms, draws her close, feels the thinness of her, her bones so obvious under the veneer of skin and muscle. He wants to feed her eggs and tomatoes, watch her dip toast into the sauce and grin as she smears her chin.

But she's rigid in his arms.

"Kathy," he whispers.

And that's like a jolt to her. He feels her jerk. She pulls away sharply, frowning. "Where am I?"

"You're at Union. We're going home."

He takes her hand which is cold and plastic and tugs her toward the corridor. At first she resists, glancing over her shoulder at the other whispering huddles and then puts one foot forward, another, another, following him through the corridor.

The guitarist stops playing.

"Remember we warned you," he says.

Robert ignores him and continues to gently tug his daughter out of Union, out into the night where the sodium glow of streetlights creates a netherworld landscape. He hails a cab, gently helps her to fold into the back seat, climbs in himself and directs the driver to his address.

He's beside himself with joy when he unlocks the door to his condo and ushers Kathy inside.

"Home, Killer. We're home."

* * *

Sleep is a blessed thing, he discovers. After that first night back home he's actually slept soundly, waking in the morning to find Kathy in the kitchen, making eggs and toast, coffee. He hugs her and thinks he will explode with joy when she hugs him back, flashes him a smile and orders him to sit down.

His thoughts navigate bridges and landscapes, possible strategies to integrate her back into the world, find her an identity, give her some purpose. They discuss that. In the end she says, "Let's just leave it for a bit, okay? I need to adjust. This is a bit—"

"Weird?"

"Yeah."

He accepts that, arranges to work remotely so that she doesn't feel so alone.

By the end of the week he realizes, however, that she is alone. He has closeted himself in his office, catching up on business deals and market trends, pacing with an earpiece dangling like an earring, screens displaying the properties of the ridiculously wealthy, the currency of his life. At first Kathy brings him coffee, hovers nearby. By Friday she's taken to staring out the window to the vista of Lake Ontario.

Saturday he postpones an appointment and takes her shopping. She models clothes, her smiles fewer, and when pressed for opinions on what she does and doesn't like he watches her panic rise. He ignores the cost and just puts the entire collection on his credit card and soothes her with lunch.

The imperative of a client's call takes his attention as soon as he arrives home. He apologizes and leaves Kathy to unpack her new wardrobe, squeezing her shoulders, retreating to his office. When he emerges, a full moon hovers over the lake; Kathy at the window seat, staring out into darkness, her forehead pressed to the glass.

"What is it, Killer?" he asks, coming up beside her.

"Nothing, Dad. Everything's okay."

He stands there with her for a few moments, unsure what to do, unsure what to say, and when all his other attempts to cajole her into laughter and engagement fail, he pats her shoulder and leaves her to her thoughts. She just needs time, he's sure.

Two weeks later she's screaming in the night. He rushes to her room, flinging open the door, but Kathy's not there, the bed pristine. From there he races to the living room and finds Kathy backing away from the wall of windows, hands over her open mouth.

"Kathy!" he says, rougher than he'd intended.

She whirls toward him, drops her hands from her mouth. "What have you done?" she snarls.

Shock paralyzes him. He's not sure of what, exactly, he's being accused. He's not sure about the vehemence of her anger. He glances at the windows where she'd been facing and the hair on his nape rises, the skin on his arms crawling. He should be seeing Kathy's back reflected there, just as he sees his own front. But instead he sees Kathy staring at him out of the windows, an image, a mirage surely. He's been working too hard, under too much stress. None of this has been easy.

He tries to swallow, finds his mouth is dry, scrubs his hand over his face. In that action the world rights itself. The mirage – gone. Kathy's anger – gone.

"I'm sorry I woke you, Dad," she says. "You should go back to bed. You have a busy day tomorrow."

He does. A deal's closing. Another's about to open. "You're okay?" he says.

She nods. "Go on. Everything's fine."

"If you're sure?"

She shoos him off and he turns back to bed. What did I just see? he thinks and lies there staring at the ceiling until he thinks no more.

Another week passes. He tries to get Kathy to use the pool, take a walk with him. He even suggests she might want to take a few refresher courses at UofT. She just sits in what's come to be her usual place on the window-seat, forehead to glass, staring out to the lake.

He takes a shower, finds the filleting knife on the vanity when he reaches for a towel. Wrapped in his bathrobe he replaces the knife in the block in the kitchen, queries Kathy, who's rocking and humming by the window. She looks at him.

"Why would I leave the filleting knife in the bathroom?"

"I don't know."

That flash of anger again. "You accusing me of something?"

"No." This is uncharted territory. He doesn't know what to think.

He turns to his bedroom, armours himself with shirt and trousers, logs onto his computer and clips the earpiece in place. He takes coffee and toast in his office. At noon, when he's setting up an appointment for the designer to stage a tri-level penthouse, he's shocked almost to insensibility.

At the window of his office he sees Kathy, or at least something that looks like Kathy, outside, hovering in the air, a face as feral and filled with malice as he can imagine.

"Email me the details," he says into the headpiece, disconnects and backs away from the window.

"Kathy!" he calls out and she answers from the doorway, "What is it, Dad?"

He whirls around. She's smiling, all sweetness and light. He pivots back to the window. His heart is hammering a staccato beat.

"Dad? You okay? You look as though you've seen a ghost." She laughs then. "Bad joke, Dad, sorry. Seriously, though, you okay?"

He turns back to her, watches her for a moment, then: "Yes. Just wondered if you'd thought about those courses?" He rubs at the pain in his chest.

"I'm researching them now." And she walks away to the living-room.

It occurs to him he's never seen her actually sleep, that her bed remains unwrinkled and untouched.

* * *

Eight weeks now and he's reached a point he has to leave her. A client requires some hand-holding, the personal touch. It's a deal that could mean a commission of $1.5M. You just didn't walk away from real estate like that. Kathy seems stable enough. She assures him she'll be fine for the few days he has to be in Montreal. He's not sure about his own mind, however, and so books himself onto a Via commuter train between Toronto and Montreal. He tells himself he'll be able to work on the journey, keep Kathy in communication.

As he steps into the marble grandeur of Union's main concourse, he glances over to the Tim Horton's. A woman in a red paisley kerchief sits on a stool; beside her a young woman.

He almost trips over himself when he sees her. Kathy? He stands there in the flow of morning foot-traffic, listening to the echoing of shoes, the hollow ring of disembodied voices calling out arrivals and departures. He takes a step closer, freezes again when the bag-lady turns toward him, grins and raises a brown paper cup to him. The young woman with her turns to him also. She looks like Kathy, yes. But not. He feels his heart thud painfully. There is such anger on the woman's face, such malice. He watches her mouth an obscenity and laugh. No mistaking what she said. His fear is now an iron band around his chest. It's hard to breathe. He thinks perhaps he needs to sit down, and finds himself on his knees somehow, with the weight of these past weeks hammering his chest, and she's there, his Kathy, standing over him like smoke and shadows, her face a livid thing.

She says, "I think you're waiting for at train, Dad." She sinks beside him, laughing. "The fare's been paid. Let me help you board."

Gravity

She can hear the screech owl again, a soft, tenor tremolo in the trees. It's dusk, a time of violet light when even the air stills. Her heart stills. It has been thumping, silent to all but her, the way an owl's wings beat unheard by prey. In this suspended moment she wonders if she falls, like an owl from her perch, will she be able to effortlessly push away the air once, twice, rise in disdain of gravity and glide across the meadow to that far line of maples and spruce, find the gnarled ancient beech that spreads limbs over the spring, and rest. And watch. There the spring that flows ceaselessly, deceptively, warm to invited skin even in the bitterest of winters. Will she see that face again? Will those fingers rise as liquid cascades like skin shedding? Will she be able to conquer her fear? This time? Will she?

Her tea is ready, long-since ready. Some minutes ago the machine finished sputtering hot water into her mug. She turns away from the window, lifts the cup from the platform on the beverage maker, spoons out the tea bag and adds a splash of milk. She watches clouds billow up, form and reform. She thinks of Kathy. She thinks of her mercurial nature, remembers her laughter that seemed to consume her whole body, the smile that spread across her face and defied anyone not to laugh with her.

The clouds in her cup become beige and disappear, the way Kathy's smile did. The way the light in her eyes died long before she. There were things she could see even in their virtual visits, Kathy who had hung on the edge of a black star, studying, watching, analyzing data until it became apparent analysis had slipped into a place as bizarre as the thing she studied.

There are voices here, Mom.

There are no voices.

You wouldn't know. You're not here.

No, she wasn't there.

The tea is tepid when she finally sips it. She tastes salt, swipes angrily at her cheeks.

Ridiculously, she thinks she should put on her rubber boots, throw on her coat, and shuffle her way out to the spring. It's insane for her to even contemplate doing that. Two canes to guide an arthritic cripple over muddy April terrain isn't exactly the smartest thing to do.

But, she reasons, there are perching places along the way, built long ago by Robert before Kathy died. Before he died. Before it all fell apart.

And who the hell did she have to answer to now? No one, really. There were friends who would admonish. A son half way across the world who visited via virtual once a week. But here, now, there's only her, both a freedom and a prison.

And now Kathy had come home, a sealed cylinder of ash, a relic slipping through time/space, a promise to keep.

She looks over at her worktable where the automaton remains unfinished. A grandiose toy for a child long gone. Something from a past no longer within reach. She'd gone to the trouble to niello the silver of the wings, to articulate each feather so that when the cams and gears went through their clockwork precision it would seem the owl fluffed and preened, silently, which was a trick in itself. The answer was in the serrated primary feathers of the wings. Micro-turbulence. Smaller currents. Silence. And she'd even managed to create lift, so that the owl would actually fly. No engine. No electronic control. Just the art of the clockmaker, the toymaker, someone who knew enough about physics and art to create an articulated toy. An homage to Pierre Jaquet-Droz. A gift for a child. Her child. Long gone.

She succumbs to the comfort of her bench and work familiar to her hands.

Her hands ache now and she tries to push through the pain, fitting another flexible silver feather into the grid. Under the lens the grid and the feather's pivot are monstrous. She blinks dry eyes, feels the scratch of her lids and knows she should stop, should rest. It's getting late.

The owl calls again. She thinks she should retrofit a sound box for this automaton. But for what purpose? Who is there to hear it now, to coo and gawp over the wonder of a mechanical toy?

The wire slips into place around the eye under the quill of the feather. She reaches with the long-nosed tweezers and pulls gently on the filament of wire, watches the feather lift, pivot, lets go and picks up another of the fragile, thin slivers of silver. She runs her finger over the edge, testing for ragged edges, cries out and sucks on the blood that wells. That was a stupid thing to do, she thinks, and buffs the offending burr with a fine grit pad. Children could hurt themselves on shoddy workmanship like that.

What children? There would be no more children to explore this toy, this elaborate toy more suited to a collector than a child. What had she been thinking all those years ago?

She'd been thinking of laughter, of a way to coax laughter from that sullen, brooding daughter of hers, something of wonder to lift her from depression, maybe cause a spark of curiosity so that she'd want to investigate the real-world inspiration behind this automaton.

A promise of freedom. A promise of a flight of imagination.

But no. Instead a relic, a beautiful ornament collecting dust on a shelf high and beyond interest, until it became a weapon.

What have you done? And a labour of love then wreckage on the floor.

I knew it would hurt you.

And it had. And remained a hurt.

Too much to think about. Too much time gone.

She rises from the table, presses on the oozing cut and shuffles to the porch where she drapes a shawl around her shoulders and eases onto the swing.

The screech owl calls again, that low, warbling sound that casts such a pall of sadness into the dimming light. There is no other birdsong now, no requiem to the day. They are afraid. There is an owl awake and soon on the hunt, an owl looking out for the fledglings which are assuredly in the treeline. She knows that call. And once again wishes she could fly like those silent, grey spectres.

With her toe she pushes against the porch deck, sets the swing into motion, pushes again, watches the light fade, listens to the owl, thinking of Kathy, of Robert, of the automaton and silver niello feathers.

She should have been more careful.

Feathers can cut.

Push.

Too many feathers like that and wings could cut.

Push.

A beak as sharp as honed steel.

Push.

Talons like perfect scimitars.

And the freedom of flight. To rise.

There is pain in her foot, pain in her hip, pain throbbing in fingers abused this day with too much fine work. That feather. The cut. She tastes metal in her mouth, looks at her finger, sees the bristling of a sliver in the cut, pulls at it in the almost non-existent light, going by touch more than sight. A flare of pain. She pulls at the nub of the sliver, cries out. Finds an entire silver feather embedded in her finger. In horror she shakes her hand. Silver feathers spill from her fingertips. She brushes at them, finds feathers up her arms, feels her shoulders hunch and thicken, her legs shorten. Suddenly the world takes on clarity. Things are so defined. She raises her arms against fear, toward wonder, hears rustling in the grass, whispers in the woods. Before she thinks she's on the grass and beating her arms-become-wings against the prison of the earth, rising, rising, such silence, turns her head, sees the screech owl in the bowl of the old beech. Banks, turns. Flight! This is flight! And she dives into the trees, swooping through branches, relishing the speed, the rush of wind over feathers.

Freedom! Freedom from pain. Freedom to move. Freedom to leave the past and all its heartache behind. Kathy crushed on the edge of a gravitational singularity, her ashes slipped through the continuum back to earth. Back to her mother who outlived a daughter sliding through space. How did it come to that?

She pushes her wings down against gravity. Gravity the enemy. Gravity the magnificent wonder.

And finds her foot on the floor of the porch.

The screech owl descends from the cover of the beech and slides over the meadow. In a moment a small parliament follow.

So not metamorphosis. Just dream. And the imperative of the prison of the earth and memory, and pain in her body, in her heart.

She rises and returns to her workbench, lifts another feather and affixes the delicate wire to the automaton.

Wendy

Nothing about the day indicated anything extraordinary. By now she knew by rote the course of her life, her very long life, though from time to time—as now—she wondered how long she would be cursed with the care of certain individuals who, for a time, walked the path she trod. Wise women and queens, shamans and kings, mothers, fathers, the wounded and wandering—she'd known them all, offered comfort and succor, advice and sometimes release. And where it all began was but dim history lost among the migrating tribes fleeing relentless cold for the promise of green and arable land. A gift and a curse handed from one custodian to another.

It was not without hesitation she gave board to these Wessexmen come crashing at her door. Wild, hard men. Men with blood dried beneath their ragged nails, rust on the helms they dragged from their heads. She'd only recently undertaken to operate an inn, seeking honest living with her man away and few hands left to tend fields repeatedly ravaged by Dane and Norseman, Wessexmen and bandits thrown in for good measure. Didn't matter what the allegiance, as far as she was concerned. Men abroad these days were all little better than cut-throats and thieves. She had little heart for any of them. But she determined to take their coin.

"You're the alewife, then?" one of them asked, a tall, gruff man with a way of looking at you she was sure would be discomfiting for some. Most assuredly for a woman. But then she was not any woman and so she returned his gaze unabashed, without what was expected of her.

She nodded, unwilling to give him more, this man who was plainly the leader among these burly brutes. She's seen their like before come ravening through St. Albans.

"Then bring us ale. My men and myself are thirsty."

"Not before you've supped." She wiped the sweat from her hands on her apron, waved off the boy who scurried in to add peat to the fire.

"You dare rather greatly, alewife."

"I'll dare what I please in my own house where I am beholden to no man. And I'll see your coin before I serve you aught."

He laughed then, a great horse-snort, followed by his three men. "And does the alewife have a name that I might address her with greater civility than she has yet to show her liege."

"I know of no such liege, for I have sworn fealty to none; and if it pleases, you shall call me Mistress Gwendolyn."

"Then bring us board, Mistress Gwendolyn, and bring us ale. As it happens I have purse this day for we have taken back the Danegeld." And with that he thumped down a leather satchel that scrunched satisfactorily with metal. Coin, she assumed. Apparently coin taken from Guthrum, that heathen Dane, and this only a meagre sum of it.

Take his coin she would, and gladly, given this coin had been hard-wrung from good working folk like herself. "I'll have a silver penny for each of you to cover your board and lodging each day of your stay, paid in advance." She watched this self-proclaimed king raise an eyebrow to that, but she cared aught for the outrageousness of her demand. If he were to stay here, she would have surety she could repair whatever ill he brought down on her house. "My mattresses are of good stuff, clean straw with lavender to ward against lice, woollen blankets to keep away the cold, and sheets of linen, coarse but serviceable, laundered daily unlike most. I keep a clean house, and a modest but serviceable board." She held out her hand into which this king placed three coins of good silver, amid the grunts and protestations of the men with him. She nodded, turned on heel and shot over-shoulder, "And I'll not have my servants abused nor taken advantage. Defy me on this and you'll find it's more than the menfolk of Wessex who practice at and are good with a bow."

She heard the snorts of derision, silenced quickly she knew by this man they served. She knew who he was. But she'd pay him no homage until he'd proven he could bring to her country what he promised besides rapine and want as a piece in a game among adult boys.

To her surprise they stayed a fortnight, each morning Alfred laying down three silver pennies without ceremony or objection. By the third day the men with him left. He spent much of the day walking the grounds she kept, stooping to weed her garden, offering up cuttings of herbs. He said aught. He went hunting in the woods which bordered her hides of land, striding into her kitchen with a brace of coney one day, and once a string of pheasants which she had her cook hang and later lard and roast for his pleasure.

One evening he joined her at the small yard off the kitchen where she gave the day's leavings to the poor who came begging, fine or foul. There were enough wanting she felt it only proper to offer up this small comfort that might see them through another day. God's service and the intrusion of the local priest were not tolerated.

When she gave the gate to one such robed visitor, Alfred queried her about that.

"The way I see it, God isn't much interested in common folk, and is but a convenience when it suits them to men such as you. What I serve those in want is from the labour of the folk under my care and my own hands."

He only nodded at that, and seemingly having reached a decision, took the ladle from her hand and filled the treen held out by a lad too young to be strong-armed into Alfred's service. She watched this man who dreamed of a united country called Englaland, marked the subtle difference these few days had made, and was pleased.

By the close of the fortnight when his men returned full of news and agitation, she was in the kitchen overseeing a stew and coarse cakes on the baking stones of the hearth. Alfred sat near as had become his custom, saying aught, listening gravely to the news his men brought.

At the end of it he looked up at her, raised a brow. "Eddington then."

She nodded, gave her attention back to the cakes and turned them. He'd discussed his plans, his hopes that by defeating Guthrum once and for all at Eddington he could then force upon his rapacious Danish foe the mantle of God and thereby yoke him with a peace treaty it would bankrupt Guthrum to break. To her surprise he'd even asked her opinion. Which she gave, which in turn surprised him.

He looked back to his men. "Eddington then."

"So we prepare the fyrd?"

He nodded. They left.

And at dawn he did likewise, embracing her as a kinswoman and the words, "I fear, Mistress Gwendolyn, you will forever be bound by your skill as a caregiver, for I have seen in you these past days a person of surpassing compassion despite your prickly exterior. Should you ever find yourself in need, you have earned my undying support."

She dared to bus him upon his grizzled cheek, grinning, and then watched him turn and take to his horse, which her lad had made ready. That she would forever be bound by her need to give succor where she could was already both a boon and a bane with which she was long familiar.

***

So her need to relocate and silence rising speculation about Mistress Gwendolyn's seeming longevity had driven her to sell off her holdings in St. Albans. She washed up now in Nottingham.

She'd married a widower who ran a respectable establishment in a warren of caves at the foot of the great castle.

But James, her husband, had been persuaded to ensure his place in heaven by offering first his soul to God on pilgrimage to the lost Holy Lands, and secondly his body to King Richard's need for fighting men. And she knew beyond doubt those men, like her good James, would be fed like meat to the butcher in an attempt to wrest Jerusalem from Saladin's control.

These priests and princes wrapped trade monopolies and profits in such cloth of white. They always had. They always would. And the work left to her and those like her was to ensure there was enough of body, mind and spirit left to carry on for the next generation, and those to come.

Thinking these things, she had not expected all these years after James had gone to find her inn a way-station for pilgrims and men at arms. And this bright day of May she certainly had not expected to see the beggar come to her door, starving and incoherent, leaning heavily upon a crude crutch, a bow slung over his shoulder, the remnants of a quiver tied to the small of his back.

Seeing his want, and indeed his need, she had her lads assist him to the inglenook, and without being told had him served a bowl of the rough stew she kept hanging over the fire. He set to the food like a starving dog. She leaned over him and gently stilled his hand. "Slowly, sir, or you'll be serving it all back."

He never stopped looking at her, set the spoon back in the bowl and put his hands to his head, leaning heavily upon his elbows on the table. She relieved him of his bow, set it on the table before him, unwrapped the tattered linen quiver from his waist and placed it beside the bow. How many times had she offered these small things to the beaten men who came wandering back home?

Her fingers lingered on the exposed tip of the yew stave where the horn nock had been set, delicately carved, a bit of frippery.

A memory then: Richard's lions, he'd said. Surely they would protect him.

She felt her heart lurch. She looked sharply to the ragged man seated at her hearth, her hand fluttering to her mouth where words caught and stumbled and then tumbled, "James, is it James, my own James come home?"

And at that he was weeping, "Gwen, I've come home, home to you, home," tears scouring the dirt and grime of days, perhaps years, on this weary road back to her, and hers with his, and surprise deep inside for she'd not thought herself capable of love, not after all that interminable time long before James.

She had him taken to their own bed in a room made comfortable with tapestries on the stone walls, the exorbitance of glazing in the lite facing west where the late afternoon sun warmed the rock. A fire was quickly laid upon the hearth, a brazier of sweet herbs set to tinder, and the sheepskins piled upon him after she'd bathed him herself in a copper she'd had set in the chamber.

His wounds were great, sores suppurated, a shin bone shattered and beyond repair. He would die, she knew. Even all her skill could not keep him. And in truth she did not wish it. She's seen that look too many times: suffering, a wish for death to take them quickly. She knew her duty now, knew his need. And at dawn the next day she kissed his cold lips, tossed the wooden cup and its sleep-filled bitter dregs upon the fire, and rode away from the inn for the last time, a wanderer yet again.

***

There were new ships in the roads, come up they said from the Channel fleet and awaiting orders. She watched from the widow's walk of The George as lighters and jolly boats wove round hulls. There would be officers seeking lodgings, their stewards making arrangements. Among them, she knew, were those who would require a willing ear and a kind voice.

Later that evening she served Capt. John Elphinstone herself. His officers from the Magnificent shared board before the fire, animated, plainly relieved to be given shore leave. But Elphinstone chose to occupy the booth in the back, away from warmth and conviviality. When she set the great pie down before him he said nothing.

"More claret, Captain?"

He merely nodded and she poured; then, as he made no motion to serve himself, she cut into the crust of the coffin and laid on his plate the savoury layers of rabbit and venison, kidney and mushrooms, and thereto ladled sauce thick and redolent.

"I think you should try to eat a little, Sir," she said, not unkindly, and aware the man kept his own company for good reason. "It is likely you won't have this opportunity for long."

He looked up at her sharply.

"If I may ask, will you be journeying to your home while ashore?"

He looked down then, a frown on his brow, and she feared she'd pushed too hard. It was a delicate thing to know what to ask and when, when to push and when to pull. She'd seen enough of captains and comrades to know the weight they often bore, the sacrifice they made. The good ones at least. There were enough of the other.

"Never more," he said, not much more than a whisper, a hoarse one at that.

"I apologize for intruding. Please excuse me, Captain. I shall leave you to your supper and your thoughts."

She stepped back on her heel, ready to turn, knowing he would invite her to share his board, which he did, to bridge the gap between time and memory, which she also did, watching as he finally ate, the sauce congealed, the crust on his plate a sop. She poured him more claret and watered it judiciously, murmuring to her staff to bring a gooseberry fool, and later cheese and the last of the dried apples from fall.

He told his tale slowly, with careful prompting: a man long at sea, a bride put up in the great stone house of his father. A child stillborn, and the mother with her, the father following thereafter from a fever brought on by a virulent case of the ague. All news brought to him on the last mail packet. Old news by then.

And at last he said, "I fight a war no one here knows about nor cares. My life has gone on without me, all those I've loved lost.

And next week I lose my only other love. They are putting the Magnificent out of commission. I and the crew are to be paid off."

So what was left for a man of the sea, a man battered by hardship and decision, weary beyond reprieve? He asked her that, and she murmured hope, arranged for him a bath in her inn's finest room, a fire upon the hearth. It was not for his purse she did so. It was for his spirit, for one did not send such a one off in the morning to face Whitehall and the implacable face of bureaucracy without some recourse to compassion. Such a wound as his would find healing from no surgeon, nor stitch, nor bandage.

In the morning, when he came to pay his bill she attended him herself, waiving any fee. He protested, as she expected, for pride perceived a slight, but in her softest tone she said, "It is my honour to have served you, Captain. Should your meeting with Whitehall not be to your satisfaction, please do return to The George. My rooms are always open to you, sir, as is my ear."

He flushed at her forthrightness, but she knew he would return, if not directly from Whitehall, then at some later time.

It was, by now, a familiar pattern.

***

"I won't be long."

"You'll be forever."

"The blink of an eye."

"I'll be changed."

"I'll still love you."

"You won't remember me."

And she knew he wouldn't. Black pilots didn't. Singularity syndrome. But it helped them to think they had someone waiting, made the dive through black holes easier, caused less confusion on the return dive. She kissed him farewell and watched him go, turned back to the inn.

There was always the inn. Always the people who touched her

life, whose lives she touched. From the time she'd walked in on herself, the cave walls glowing with the paintings she'd recorded of her journeys. Names streamed by, events, a Scots playwright who'd immortalized her in his writing after she'd allowed him time and a place to grieve; an engineer from HMS Gloucester after the Battle of Jutland when she'd kept a hotel on Scapa Flow. He'd been one she'd nursed for some time after he'd been released from hospital, wounds both seen and not. That collier captain who'd risked his life that unforgettable day of June 4, 1940. A long night that. Words unsaid. Hopes unspoken. And relief when he'd returned with his charges, her inn turned to hospital and she in the background offering her own special form of succor. So many over the years. Women escaping husbands. Children in want of bread.

It was difficult not to become hard of heart. It was difficult not to shed tears in stolen private moments when no one could hear, and no one could see. And always the thought: when will it end? When will my long life of service release me?

Now here. The way-station she'd come to shepherd for the captains who returned unknown to themselves, men and women, lost souls, her lost boys.

She watched the woman walk into the small foyer she kept. No staff now. Not in some time. She could tell this one was fresh from a black dive and unsure of herself and her surroundings, staring out of the windows of St. John's port to the spectacle beyond. This captain would be staying awhile. It was there in the tick in the woman's right eyelid, the way it drooped, the way she kept leaning, as though stretching, reaching.

"Welcome to Wendy's Inn," she said, and watched the woman turn to her and surrender.

A Perfect Spell

I watched him from the study window, his measured gait, the afternoon sun at his back. It was always the same. He was a nimbus. The winding track to my tower unravelled behind him like a golden thread, Lac du Bras d'Or an earth-bound star in the distance. I wondered if the outcome of his approach would be any different this time. Doubtful. For how many years had I watched this apprentice arrive at my gate, heard the insistent bell toll his presence, listened as the porter rebuffed his request.

He always gained entry. It was part of the relentlessness of time, of this destiny I'd unwittingly cast for myself.

"Why do you keep trying, Master?" Dilys asked. I heard the edge in his voice, the disapproval.

"Because I must," I answered, keeping my back to him. "Where is Efa?"

"She's in the herb room."

I laughed at the absurdity of it. "You disobeyed me."

"I didn't see the point in obeying." The bell jangled again, insistent, demanding. This time the porter's voice rose sharply to my window

– I said the Master isn't taking any apprentices. Go away! – and then the clang of the sally-port.

"Last time I checked, Dilys, I was the master of this holding."

"And I'm your steward, Master. I take care of you."

"By disobeying my orders?" Again the bell rang. Why wouldn't this fellow just go away? But of course I already knew the answer. "Do you care so little for your daughter?"

"You know as well as I trying to send him away will change nothing. Just as trying to send away Efa will serve nothing. It is futile. How many times have we done this, Master? The book is powerful. The spell is powerful."

He was, of course, quite right. We'd tried everything over the years, even centuries, to change this day, and despite everything, despite reason and study and all the weight of this body of knowledge I'd acquired, nothing – absolutely nothing – turned aside that hand of fate. Gerreint would apprentice to the master of this tower. His manners would be impeccable, his intelligence keen. And he would seal his fate, yet again, into this mobius coil.

I turned my back to the window and slumped into the chair at my desk, glaring at the ancient book open upon the lectern. "Tell the porter to let him in, Dilys. I am sick to my soul of this."

* * *

My last patient stared at the linen and plaster binding his forearm. It was clear from the look on his leathery face he thought this a waste of rare and expensive materials. I hummed something tuneless while I trussed his arm into a sling. Between that and the fragrance of myrrh from the brazier, there was enough strangeness to reinforce the legends about me, I was sure. Of course, the book and lectern that followed me from room to room didn't help. The wizard in his tower. The Book of Enoch. It was too easy to dazzle them with a few phrases of Latin and a waggle of fingers. They tolerated me, these rough miners and farmers, ancient Gaels all of them. I healed their sick, set their bones, and sometimes I offered services outside of their dour and pitiless religion, services that harkened back to their elders' legends. Between that and my association with the Mi'kmaq, and facility with the resettled Acadiennes, they feared me enough to let me work whatever it is I did in this wizard's tower.

Wizard's tower indeed. It's amazing what can be done with a ruin of a silo, a little imagination and coin enough to buy labour, and sometimes silence.

"You're out of the mines for the next month," I told him. "Don't use that arm. Come back and see me at the end of the term. I'll remove the cast. If you follow my orders your arm will be fine and your household secure."

"And until then what are we to do for our bread?"

It was always the question. My response was always the same. "See the porter. Arrangements will be made." I gave him a sharp look, forestalling his objection. "It's not charity. It's insurance. If you die from starvation how am I to collect a fee in future?" I helped him into his shirt and waistcoat, let Efa come back into the room to take care of the rest.

She breezed past me, clucking soothing sounds to the miner. Her lack of acknowledgement to me was as much an accusation as a shout of anger. We'd quarrelled earlier. It was the same argument: she wouldn't leave; she wouldn't try to change the course of our destiny. Why try to correct the perfect spell that held we three suspended in time? Why when nothing so far had worked? Why not just admit defeat, bow to the brilliance of my work, and accept fate?

I watched her for a moment, remembered when what she and I shared was new and fresh and aflame as that cascade of red curls that tumbled down her back. I felt the ache of it again, that lost love, that lost youth. It was then I realized youth was a state of mind, not a measure of numbers.

There was a steady maritime drizzle when I left the building that housed the herb room and infirmary. It always seemed to me the clouds simply swallowed the island. By the time I gained my study in the tower, a haze of moisture clung to my clothes. Dilys waited for me. So did the book. There was warmed wine on the table. He sat near the blaze on the hearth, bent over his knees. He didn't look up when I came in.

"Gerreint's settled in," he said. "He's waiting to see you."

"Let him wait." I swallowed some of the wine, let its warmth spill through my limbs.

"What are you going to do this time?"

"I'm not sure." I set the cup on the desk, watched Dilys. The man, like me, hadn't aged a day in all our long years. His fate, like Efa's, was caught up in the knowledge of the book, of words spoken aloud and in vain, a trio, a trinity, spinning through time. It's what happens when you've created the perfect spell, the perfect solution to mortality. "Any ideas?"

"We should all kill ourselves."

"If you recall, we tried that solution once."

He barked a laugh. I could hear the despair in it.

"Why did you have to meddle?" he asked. "Why did you have to mess with things you aught not? What was wrong with dying?"

That old argument. The accusation. The wish to undo the calamity that followed my arrogance.

"Because I could," I answered, as always. "Because I loved her." After all this time there was no point attempting to disguise what had been my hunger, the thing that drove me to scour every ancient text that might have contained the original Book of Enoch, said to contain the whereabouts of the Book of Life. It was this latter book, and its counterpart, the Book of Death, that was the focus of my obsession. One recorded the name of every person who would live. The other recorded the name of every person who would die.

Ask enough questions, get to know the right people, and eventually you arrive at your destination. Proof of that sat in this room. And the recipe for that result lay open for anyone to see on the lectern.

"I miss Alexandria," he said. He straightened, arched his back and dragged the cap from his head. "I miss the noise and the smell and heat. How I miss the heat."

"Not a very good Orkney man."

"Still."

"You know why I couldn't stay. You know why I had to find somewhere away from the world to research and hide. You didn't have to—"

"Follow. I know. So much for loyalty. And love. She wouldn't listen, you know that." Dilys looked at me then. I felt the weight of that look. "It's not so much for myself, but for Efa. She's too young to be caught in this."

It was my turn to laugh. The thought of Efa being too young was about as absurd as our situation. "I think you better send in Gerreint."

"Of course." Dilys crossed to the door, hesitated. "Isn't it strange? Meeting him again?"

"Always. Like looking in the mirror."

* * *

Gerreint made it clear he understood the terms of his apprenticeship, although he also made it clear he didn't think much of having to tend to the needs of the patients in the infirmary. Changing sheets and scouring bed pans wasn't quite what he had in mind, he let me know. Neither was trekking across the heath and spruce around Bras d'Or his idea of studying the mysteries of life. He hadn't, he let me know, come all this way to gather bark, berries and lichen. That was work any peasant could do.

"Give me a chance, Master," he said. "I can prove myself worthy." I remembered saying exactly the same thing. But then he did say something I don't recall saying. "I've travelled all the way from the north coast of Africa to study with you."

That made me sit up. "How did you hear about me there?"

"A book merchant spoke to me in the Khan el-Khalili. It's an old market—"

"In Cairo. I know. What did he say?"

"He said his father's father's father knew of a Welshman who had travelled across the Great Green. That he'd gone to Papay Morn to study with a great scholar and magician. There was rumour, he said, the man's descendant left the Orkneys and gone beyond, to colonies now owned by the British. He said this man was a scholar and a prophet, a man who read ancient texts and knew ancient mysteries. He said it was likely the man's descendant still lived there and might be able to help."

"And you believed him?"

"There are stranger mysteries in Cairo."

"And so you came by yourself to investigate a rumour?"

"I came alone, yes. And you're plainly no rumour."

Another new thing. And being as this day continued to be full of surprises, I thought I'd cast aside all caution and try the unknown and unproven, in light of the fact the known and proven had resulted in nothing but heartache over the years.

"You can apprentice to me," I said at length, watching firelight flicker over his worn waistcoat of brown wool. There was a hole in the knee of his hose, and the cuff of his breeches were threadbare and ravelling. I looked up at that face I knew so well, the sharp lines of cheekbones, a jaw like an axe blade, the spill of dark hair from beneath the workman's leather cap he wore like a second skull. "But first you're going to have to hear a story, and tomorrow let me know if the terms of our agreement will be acceptable. You may have the use of my study tonight." I raised my brows, waiting for his comment.

He stared at me a long moment. Outside the wind had picked up, now to a buffeting force that rattled the vines on the masonry and sucked the flames up the flu of the hearth. For answer he nodded, once only, gestured in question to the settle by the fire and when I gave him leave to sit, he did so.

It was then I risked all and told Gerreint my long story.

* * *

What started it all was when I called on the hermit of Papay Holm, having heard he was looking for an apprentice, someone to assist him in his spare life, in his study. I know, I know, you're wondering how it is I could have inquired after that now dead and legendary figure. Patience.

That first time it was my hunger for knowledge that drove me to his island and his door. It was said he could see the future in a bowl of water. It was said he had ancient scrolls from the lost library of Alexandria. It was said he tapped into the Divine. That he was also the keeper of the dead of the long dead Knap of Howar added to his legend.

What scholar could resist the temptation to learn from the mind of such a person?

That first time it had been snowing, a driving sleet that drove needles of ice into my face. I'd paid off the boatman, stood there at the end of a fiord on the Papay Holm of the Orkney Islands, facing a staircase up the northern face.

I was fifteen and cocky. Don't laugh. You're not much beyond that and you're still cocky. It comes from a lack of experience, you know. Fall down enough and you soon learn invincibility is for imbeciles. We are, none of us, invincible.

What happened over the course of the next years was the foundation for my downfall. The hermit, you see, had a steward, and the steward, in turn, was a widower with a daughter. Not much of a hermit you might think. But truth of it was the hermit spoke little. His steward saw to his needs, traded with the boatman who would sail when he could for staples and rare supplies.

When finally I gained the hermit's trust and his confidence, I lay before him the precious cargo I'd brought with me, none other than the original books referenced in the Book of Enoch. Indeed, yes, The Book of Life and the Book of the Dead. Instead of wonder and delight, he ordered the books destroyed, to be cast into the ocean. Not meant for the likes of us, he said. Not meant for mortal and fallible eyes. Terrible thought, yes, I know, to destroy such precious knowledge. You've travelled far to study that knowledge, to peer into the face of the eternal.

Wasn't it enough, I asked my mentor, that so much had been lost when Julius Caesar conquered Egypt and won her queen but lost the knowledge of the world when the great library burned? Surely he didn't wish to heap calamity upon calamity?

"The greater calamity would be to unleash upon the world the knowledge you carry," he answered. I thought he would combust he was so furious. And despite all my arguments he held to his belief the books should be destroyed. He was right, of course. But, of course, the books were not meant to be destroyed. We've tried, you see, over the years. And that hasn't worked either.

And why should we want to destroy the books, you wonder? Why advocate such heresy?

Because of the love I had for my mentor's steward's daughter. She was, is!, beautiful, a flightless bird caught on that barren rock that was no more than a grave for the dead Knap of Howar, and themselves a people long forgotten in the wind and the spray of the sea. It was a memory she served. And I thought I might free her of exile. I thought love and knowledge would liberate us all.

So I studied in secret, while my master tended to the rocks of the island. I was a perfect apprentice. I wrote his findings. I picked and dried and shelved his herbs, his roots, the rare finds on that lonely place. I tended the sick who braved the journey. I transcribed his visions when he'd scry. We worked on alchemy, on metaphysics, on the mysteries of the world. And as the weeks and months slipped away I came to understand I could manipulate even time with the right combination of actions. The key to it lay in finding the mathematical equation that resulted from the list of names omitted in the Book of the Dead. A daunting task, you say. Well what knowledge worth having isn't?

And during these years that caged bird I loved came to love me also. I thought I would die from an excess of joy. But it was she who died, swept from the rocks by a wave out of nowhere. There was no body. If the sea-witch claims you, she is a jealous guardian and does not give up her dead.

It was then I did the unthinkable. I scraped her name from the Book of the Dead. It was a last hope, an act of desperation. She showed up the next afternoon with a basket on her arm, carrying saxifrage and lingonberries. She's been doing the same thing every twenty-four years for about six hundred years.

* * *

I left Gerreint in my study long after the rest of the holding had hunkered down under wool and sheepskin coverlets. Efa was awake and in a squirrel-lined robe near the fire when I finally opened the door to my bedchamber. She sat upon a hard, ladderback chair, a horn cup held in the palms of her hands, rolling it back and forth, back and forth. She looked up when I closed the door. There were stains under her eyes, her hair a torrent of cinnamon and copper.

"I do still love you, you know," she said, her voice barely above a whisper, a ghost, a breath caught in the crackle of the fire.

I sank to the floor, laid my head on her knee. She shivered. I doubted it was for lack of warmth. "I know," I said. "I'm sorry. I'm sorry for all these years."

"Will it be different this time?"

"I don't know. I told him the truth this time."

"Well that was novel."

"He's been to Cairo, to the Khan el-Khalili. He knew about the books. That's never happened before."

"I wish I could say I was hopeful."

"I wish I could too. Come, Efa. There's no point sitting here. Come to bed."

* * *

I spent the night in that tower. My tower, I realized. Strange to think of. Made the concept of talking to oneself take on a completely new perspective. That my master (I, in fact) had been distressed earlier was plain. As incredible as the story seemed, there was logic to it, an elegance I understood.

Later, that probability and elegance proved correct when I turned the pages of the book on the lectern. It didn't require years of study and research to plumb the depths of this problem. Just look up three names. Look them up twice. Once in one book. Once in the other. Undo what had been done. Lock and seal the books away. Lock the tower. Summon the steward Dilys. Explain the importance that he and Efa meet me on the track before sunrise.

And when dawn broke behind us we stood in the hollow below the holding, Bras d'Or breathing mist, watching fire consume what I hoped was the end of a long journey that should never have begun. My mentor – my other self – agreed to stay in the tower after I explained what I'd done. He'd laughed. I think he hadn't laughed like that for a long time, because it seemed as if he'd finally found the humour in life, and, having found it, was prepared for death. He said mine was a solution he'd not considered. I'd responded that eventually we'd have come to it, as we did.

I still find it odd to think that.

Despite the cloak, I shivered. Efa slipped her hand into mine. I looked over at her, sure I loved her from the moment I saw her, sure what I'd done this time would heal the rift I'd caused centuries ago. We'd age now, all of us, let time and life lead us into the unknown, begin the adventure we should have had, the one every youth dreams and follows and changes and follows again as the path of our lives unwinds before us. Like the track to which we turned, now picked out in gold and frost, and disappeared up the rise and round the bend.

The Intersection

First published in Strangers Among Us, editor Susan Forest

Hey, Sis!"

She glanced around. His voice sounded so real inside her head, as if he stood right beside her. He sounded so ebullient amid the hustle of traffic, sunshine in the canyons of King and Bay, reaching out across distance where he circled somewhere overhead. She glanced up to where a sky like flint shone, hard as armour, and for her an unreachable barrier, untouchable. Although she wanted to reach him, one of the reasons she'd contacted him via their link.

She touched her ear as if that would allow her to be nearer him, aware of the neural communications implant lodged in her cortex, one of Jack's amazing gizmos. "Hey." She winced at the tone of her response, aware of the flatness of it, her inability to match his persistent, apparent joy.

"Where are you?"

She glanced up at the monoliths of the TD and Montreal towers where birds wheeled and dove into the verdancy of wall gardens, down to the traffic lights where a walking man flashed and a flat voice droned walk, walk, walk over the hiss of activity, electric cars, electric public transit. Someone bumped by her. She stood immobile, unable to face the paved river she had to cross.

"Going to work," she said, sucking in air suddenly in too short supply. "What are you doing?"

"Just making notations on our latest neural interface results. Being able to conduct these tests here is giving me amazing insights, things I would never have been able to ascertain down there." There was a pause, and then: "Hey, Sis, you okay?"

That question. How many times had he asked her that? And how many times had she found herself frozen with fear, incapable of answering, terrified of the answer and what that might indicate, even more terrified of not telling him and having to face the gorge below where her feet balanced precariously on the edge of sanity.

All she had to do was cross the street with the lights, walk across the courtyard of the TD Centre, into the glass atrium where commerce and a Carolinian forest grew, and from there ascend in an elevator which could take her up fifty-six floors if she wanted. But she only had to go to thirty-two, exit to a floor where she would work where she chose, in a zen garden or beanbag chair, at an oak table or a cherry-lined library filled with real, printed volumes, and there design security protocols for payment gateways.

"Sis?"

"Yeah."

"You okay? Talk to me."

She inhaled sharply, her chest constricting. She could feel her heart hammering a tattoo, her legs liquefying.

"Sis? C'mon, say something."

What was she supposed to say? That she was falling apart? Again. That the meds didn't seem to be working again, that she felt as though everything was about to come crashing down around her, that maybe it might be better to just sleep, and sleep forever, to stop being a burden to both herself and Jack. He certainly didn't need to be dealing with a whacked-out sister some three hundred kilometres back on terra firma.

"You know, you're closer up there than you were on the Rock," she said, avoiding the conversation, needing the conversation, unable to begin the conversation.

"How weird is that?" He had such a comforting bass rumble in his voice, like the sound of the earth itself.

"I know," she said.

Another pause she didn't know how to fill.

"But you didn't call me to discuss distance."

Well, sort of she did. Twenty-four hundred klicks from Toronto to Corner Brook. Three hundred to the International Space Station II. But she could hop on a plane to Corner Brook within the hour, or at least later today. But the ISSII? Jack was only as close as the voice in her head.

"Don't make me drag this out of you, Sis. C'mon, you know you need to talk. You know you need to tell me what's going on. Otherwise I can't help you."

"I know."

"So?"

"I can't get to work." There. It was out. She imagined a greedy little gremlin cavorting around her ankles, biting, nipping, making a mockery of all her anxieties and fears.

"Why? You sick?"

She blinked away the gremlin. "Just in the head."

"Now stop that. You're having a panic attack, right?"

"Yes."

"Where are you exactly?"

"Watching the lights at King and Bay."

"Why are you watching the lights?"

"Because I can't cross the road."

"Why can't you cross the road?"

"Cause I'm scared." And that tore it. Now she blinked back tears, was aware she was gasping, that pedestrians were beginning to look at her askance. It seemed the ultimate irony a homeless woman rumbled by with her cart and stink and her babble of inner dialogue. Déjà vu? Premonition?

"What are you scared of?"

"The traffic, the road, the fact the lights might change before I make it across. Of even if I make it across what if the elevators choose today to break down? Or what if there's a terrorist who's managed to infiltrate one of the towers and decides to take himself and everyone else to redemption? It happens, you know. You're up there circling around while down here there are crazies all over the place." And one in particular standing immobile at the corner of King and Bay trying to cross the road to work.

"Last I heard there hadn't been any terrorist attacks in Canada for some number of years, and even those were isolated incidents perpetrated by disturbed people. So I don't think the elevators are going to blow up and take out the tower."

Disturbed people. She was a disturbed people. "But what happens if I get stuck in the road when the lights change?"

"Well, it's not like motorists are going to gun their engines and run you down because you didn't make the lights."

"But they'll be angry."

"Maybe. Fuck them. Just continue on. And it's unlikely you're going to get stuck in the middle of road."

"Not unless I freeze."

"Have you ever done that?"

"No."

"Well there you go."

"There's always a first time."

"So, what, you're going to plant yourself in the middle of the crossing just to prove there's always a first time you won't make it across the road?"

Despite herself, she could feel the corner of her mouth twitch in response to his humour. "I'm not that crazy."

"You're not crazy, Sis. Sure, you have issues, problems we both know we need to monitor and work through. But so do lots of people, whether it's physical or physiological. We're all gloriously flawed. Show me a perfect person, and I'll show you a biological android."

"Yeah, maybe."

"Yeah, maybe nothing. So, your heart palpitating?"

"Ready to freakin' jump out of my chest."

"Ah, Sis is channelling Alien."

She snorted a laugh. "That would freak people out."

"Yeah, so let's work on that, shall we? You taking long, slow breaths?"

She inhaled deeply, let it go. "Yes."

"Now go to your safe place."

"What? Here?"

"Sure, why not."

"It will look weird."

"I've got you on SAT right now and you don't look weird at all. Awesome doo, by the way. When did you decide to shave your head and do tats?"

She looked up at the sky again, amazed he could zero in on her from so far away. She glanced back down to the streetscape, shuffled over to the bench at the transit stop and eased onto it, aware how weak her legs were, how her hands fluttered like frightened birds.

"Good move, Sis. Very good. Now, where are you in your head?"

She closed her eyes. The sounds around her distilled into a susurration not unlike waves on a cobble beach. Agawa. A moonrise, huge, white, hanging over a promontory that lay darkly like a sleeping giant.

"Superior," she said. "Our last summer there." Before Jack had gone off to university, and she had to navigate the uncharted waters of secondary.

"That was epic."

She heard the wistfulness in his voice, felt it herself. Life had been so simple then. "I will never forget that summer."

"Me neither."

"Remember how cold the water was?"

"Bloody nut-cracking."

She laughed.

"And you swam circles around me, and then dragged me out of the water because my lips had turned blue."

"Yeah, I did, didn't I?"

"Cause we always took care of each other."

She nodded, sucked in a breath to still tears.

"Listen, Sis, you're gonna feel a lightness in your head in a sec. Don't freak, okay? It's just me uploading a modification to your implant."

Her eyes flew open, panic slamming through her. Even as she uttered: "Not here, Jack! Please!" she felt a tingling in her head, like a cold itch she couldn't scratch, and then she was on her feet, gulping air, Jack's voice crooning gently, "It's okay, Sis. Honest. You know I'd never do anything to hurt you. Really, you're gonna love this. Almost done. You with me?"

"Uh-huh." And then the sensation stilled, and there was only the sound of wind again as vehicles drove by, of the birds, of other pedestrians chatting either to each other or through their own earpieces. The bus sighed to a stop in front of her, the doors opening, passengers spilling out, sweeping up. "What did you do?"

"A modification that will help, I think. Something I've been working on. You're my first trial subject. Not exactly protocol, but, hey, you fit the profile." She heard him laugh. "Now, c'mon, Sis. You remember how when we were little Mom always told me to take your hand when we crossed the street, that it was my responsibility to make sure you arrived safely on the other side?"

So many roads crossed, Jack holding her hand. So many. Her fingers tingled, and then her palm, and she felt warmth there in her left hand, felt the pressure of a hand, of fingers tightening around hers.

"So, I'm still going to hold your hand, Sis."

She felt fingers squeeze. She looked up sharply at the sky again. "Jack?"

"Yep, that's me."

"But—"

"How?"

"Yeah."

"Does it really matter?"

She looked down at her hand, the way her own fingers curled around his which weren't there, but were. "No."

"Then, c'mon. Let's cross the intersection."

The lights had changed again, walk, walk, walk droning across King and Bay, and tentatively, her hand in Jack's, she stepped out into the intersection and walked to the courtyard, the atrium, and into the elevator to work.

Civil Liberties

The first time I asked Mom for my own communication link she said, "No, son. Isn't gonna happen."

Two weeks later, I'm sitting at the table, eating chapatis and bhindi bhaji, and tried again. "Please, everyone at school has their own."

"Everyone at school is rather encompassing."

"Well, lots of kids do."

"You're not lots of kids. No, I'm sorry."

"But —"

"I said no."

I knew that tone. And I knew that look. I'd go think about this and come back with something better. I couldn't help but wonder, though, what she meant by you're not lots of kids, and the thought she saw me the way they did – well, that stung. Even though I was supposed to be a big all-fired secret, the whole station knew what I was. Friggin Pinocchio. Adopted son of a geneticist. Nano-man.

"I've got a treat for you," she said.

"Oh?" I refused to look at her. I could hear the clatter of dishes as she loaded them into the sanitizer. I scooped up the last mouthful of bhindi and put my plate in the rack. There was a sunset glow from the holo over the sink. A bluejay zoomed onto the branch of the pine, its sharp fluting call carrying through our apartment. I wondered why Mom clung to these images from Canada. I'd much rather see the crisp shapes of Saturn and her moons. "What's the treat?" I asked.

"We have to go to the lab for it."

I felt dinner go sour. "Not another test."

She draped her arm around me and squeezed. "No, Dulal, I promise. This is definitely a treat. Bit of a secret, but a treat."

"Well, why do we have to go to the lab?"

She laughed. "You'll see. C'mon, gloomy guts. You're gonna love this."

I tapped in the cycle for the sanitizer. "Whatever. Yeah, okay."

Once out in the corridor we cut through to the arboretum where evening light sifted through the trees. I always wondered why there were no kids here in the evening, unlike the deck above where execs and miners lived. Off the path, some guy sat cross-legged on the ground, a hang drum cradled in his knees. His fingers danced over the shining dome of the drum, music like bells filling the air, a woman dancing with ribbon wands making streams of colour around her. From there we swung off to the right and to the airlock, the sound of the hang fading.

"Damn," Mom said. I looked back at her, wondered what was up, and then saw two miners approaching with a woman in a white helmet. "We'll have to wait. Must be a problem with the water extractors from Enceladus." We retreated a few paces.

"What makes you say that?"

The outer airlock hissed shut, enclosing the trio. I watched as they punctuated their conversation with gestures, watched them move through to the second stage.

"That's one of the chief engineers with them," Mom said.

"Figure it's a big deal?"

"Probably not. It's a pretty good team they have on the station. Ah, there, they're through. C'mon, our turn."

We stepped into the airlock, waited for the signal to move through to the next section where we transported in the lift to the research ring, four decks beyond.

"Do you miss it, Mom?" I asked, thinking about the guy with the hang drum, about the trees in the arboretum.

"Miss what?"

"You know. Earth. Canada. The pines you have on our holos."

She looked down at me. Lights from the deck levels slid over her face, bright and dark, bright and dark. "What makes you ask that?"

"I dunno. I just thought that maybe you missed it cause you're not from here."

She frowned a moment. "Yeah, sometimes. But the work I do here is so important." Her fingers touched my cheek. "And you're here. How could I miss Earth for long with you here?"

We took C Corridor when we docked, each of us going through security checks. Unlike the residential deck, the research deck formed a series of pads like lollypops that stuck out from the core, connected by airlocks. The first thing I noticed that was different were the walls of green plants, dripping with white flowers and red fruit. Mom gestured widely, grinning.

"Strawberries," she announced.

I looked at her, trying to figure out what the big deal was. So they'd made a wall of plants. Yeah, that was a big deal, for sure, but she seemed to think this was something I should get excited about. I shrugged.

She laughed and picked one of the dangling berries. "Try this."

"Eat it?"

"No. Play catch with it. Yes, eat it, silly." She popped one in her mouth. Geez she was all weird about this, closing her eyes, making weird noises.

I took a nibble of the end of the fruit. Wow! Popped the whole thing in my mouth and chewed. Wow! There was all this sweet juice, and the taste was, well, like amazing!

She laughed again, watching me. "I know, eh? They're strawberries. We had samples in suspension and decided they might be a safe thing for our self-sufficiency program." She gestured to the long corridor of hanging green plants. "They're easy to grow. We've hybridized them, obviously, so they're self-pollinating, give a high yield, and can tolerate the light conditions here. And what's even better is they don't take up much room and can be grown in common spaces, increasing the biodiversity of the station, and the nutritional value of our diet." She looked back at me. "Cool, huh?"

I had to admit it was amazing. I picked another berry and chewed away. Mom joined me. It was the best dessert of my life.

A week later I'm sitting in my World Politics class at school. We'd been studying civil liberties for the past two weeks – a yawn for most of us, but following the thoughts of Thoreau, Paine, as well as the modern libertarians Vanderkemp and Bhatnagar, made me realize the solution to the problem of my own communication link lay not in appealing to Mom's maternal instincts, but rather to her intelligence.

And why was it so important I have my own link? Well, time for one thing. I mean here I was, trying to shove together this essay, and I limped through the slowest downloads you can imagine from our local station access. My tablet's sitting there on the desk in front of me, that little spinner just swirling around and around. Enceladus could have been sucked dry before I'd finally download the information I wanted. In the meantime, Jeevika sitting beside me not only accessed five solar sites through her link, but downloaded clips and tunes at the same time. I mean, it was embarrassing! Even frustrating!

So, that evening I'm sitting cross-legged on the floor of our common room, once more trying to download some research for this stupid assignment. Mom was stretched out on the sofa, reader hanging in front of her. I could see her face through the projection. I figured now as good a time as any to hit her with another try.

"You know, Mom, it's an infringement of my civil liberties to deny me my own link."

She arched a brow, but didn't even look at me when she said, "Nice try. And how, exactly, have I infringed upon your civil liberties?"

"You're denying me my personal freedom of expression and research," I answered. "I have the right to pursue research uncensored, unmonitored. You talk about this sort of thing all the time about your work."

That made her look over at me. The reader did a horizontal to her belly. In the background I could hear the music shuffle to classic guitar.

"We can't afford it."

"I thought you wanted me to study hard, to learn, to explore."

"I do."

"Then we have to find a way."

"How, Dulal? These things are expensive. And in case you hadn't noticed I'm not a miner or an engineer connected to the mining facility. I'm just a genetic biologist."

"Is it because of what I am?" There it was. Out in the air between us.

"You're my son, Dulal."

"And I'm a freak."

That made her sit up. "Says who?"

"Everyone knows I'm NanoMan."

"NanoMan? Where did that come from?"

I couldn't look at her. If I did I was sure I'd cry. "Doesn't matter."

She slid down off the sofa and pulled up my chin, "You listen to me, Dulal. You may not have been created in my womb. But you were completely from biological sperm and my egg. You may have a nano-structure that assists your DNA. But you are all mine. You're most definitely my son."

"But the kids all say the reason I don't have my own link is because I'm property."

Mom got up then. I thought she was pissed. All her movements were sharp and short. She was keying something into her Personal Communications Device (PCD), muttering the whole time. I ran the back of my hand across my eyes, angry that I'd allowed myself to cry, that I'd made her upset.

My own PCD warbled then. I thumbed the message and gawped, looked over at Mom who had her own tears and a frown. I looked back down at the message there. It was a ridiculous sum of money she'd transferred to me.

"No kidding?" I said. "Wow, no kidding?" I looked back to Mom. "But you said we couldn't afford it."

"That's right."

"But so where does this credit come from?"

"It's our household budget for the next month."

That brought my attention to full alert. "But what will we live off of?"

"I can manage to fudge things for about thirty days with most accounts. Food credits, though, are going to be difficult."

"Food credits? But –"

"—How will we eat?" I nodded. "Well, everything we have stocked will be allocated for you, because you're the youngest and if I don't make sure you're properly housed, clothed and fed, the station authorities could take you away from me."

"They'd do that?"

"It's part of what you called your civil liberties. Children must be cared for. You know very well it's a big freaking deal for families with children to be allowed to live on the station."

"But what about you?"

"Oh, I'll manage. I can scrounge some stuff from the lab, eat lots of strawberries," She flicked a smile. "And people are always leaving lunches in the lab fridge."

"But that's stealing!"

"It's surviving. But you'll have the link, and that's more important. But what concerns me is paying for our air allotment, and the intravenous anti-viral boosters, because that I can't juggle."

"But we can't survive without air, and what if we start a new contagion?!"

"I know."

"But that means we'd have to live in public spaces!"

"I know."

"And that's illegal. The station doesn't allow vagrants."

"I know."

"But we'd be homeless, Mom!"

"But you'd have your link, and I don't want you to do without your civil liberties, Dulal. You know you mean everything to me, that I'd walk through fire for you. There are places we could hide out."

"But they'd take me away from you! That happened to one kid whose mom was a miner on the asteroid." And what rules there might be about me, because Mom had engineered me into a kid who would stand a better chance in space, I had no idea. I tried very hard to keep a calm face, to breathe normally, and I wanted so much to go and hug Mom and hear her say all would be well. Damn, this was hard!

I thumbed my PCD. I could hear Mom's chime. She flicked the air to open it.

"You cancelled the transfer?" she asked.

I nodded and fled to her, hugging her. "I don't need my civil liberties at the expense of other people."

She gulped at that and hugged me back fiercely. But of course neither of us were crying. Not really.

A Bear at the Fridge

First published in Polar Borealis, Issue 6

Perhaps the real question was whether she should just cut any attempt at logic, and go directly to a nervous breakdown. Maybe she should start shouting into the middle of this weird night. Or declaim the existence of spirits and guides, and what the hell was this bear—a grizzly no less—doing slurping Coke from her fridge. Standing up slurping Coke from her fridge. Smiling no less. Even offering some pretty interesting conversation, were she honest, around prodigious belching.

By now Ralph—that was his name, so he insisted—was on his sixth Coke, which was reasonable she supposed when she thought about it. He was, after all, a prodigious great beast of a bear, so six cans of brown fizz didn't seem so extreme.

Extreme? She was thinking about the ramifications and quantification of extreme when there was this—

She grabbed the tea towel hanging from the stove and held it up against herself, realized that wee pocket handkerchief of a tea towel wasn't going to do anything to cover boobs and crotch, and then wondered why she bothered because the bear—Ralph—

wouldn't be concerned she was standing there gawping like some great beached fish, naked as new. She hung the towel over her shoulder. Seemed like a good thing to do.

Behind Ralph, the microwave displayed 3:31 in cool blue light. Of the bloody AM!

Maybe I'm hallucinating? Dreaming? Maybe I'm really still in bed.

"So the thing is," Ralph said, "I'm getting kind of tired chasing you around in your dreams, so I figured I'd wake you up." He shook that mammoth head and she wondered if that growl was laughter or something that meant she should turn around and make for the back door, which was closest, instead of standing there in the dimness of her kitchen, the glow of the open fridge door spilling out like a Colville painting across the tiles. Maybe she should run screaming into the night. What would Ellis and Petra think if she showed up at their front door at this hour? Naked? Burbling about bears, well one bear to be exact, drinking soft drinks in her kitchen.

Batshit crazy is what they'd think. Wonder if she'd spent too much time up in the woods alone chasing spirit guides. Or maybe was growing some hot stuff in her barn.

And then she thought: But there aren't any grizzlies here!

Not in Ontario, that was for sure. Certainly not up on the Bruce. Black bears sure.

And no bloody grizzlies discussing climate change in front of your fridge door!

Well, dream or no, what did this bear, this Ralph, want with her? Chasing her around in her dreams? Had she been dreaming of bears? Of grizzlies? And Coke? Seriously?

But then as she watched him leaning on the fridge door, she did remember vague images of bears, or a bear to be precise. A bear trying really hard to squeeze into the palm of her hand. Just the way a spirit guide might. She looked at her left hand, turned it palm up, felt it itching, looked back at up Ralph—why was it so easy to call him that?—and wondered how some talking ursine could shrink enough to fit into her hand. Or for that matter, how he could pass through skin and bone and muscle and stuff and get inside her.

She shuddered.

Ralph shook his head and whuffed again, his jaw waggling. She was sure that was laughter.

This was absurd. She backed away, out onto the porch, grabbed the throw on the old rocker and threw it around her shoulders. She thought maybe she should sit down. Her knees were by now yelling at her to do that, to bend over, to swim out of the greyness buzzing at the edges of her sight, but instead she leaned back, felt the hard spindles against her head, the cool zephyr coming down off the hills. Cricket song. The night. The sanity of this place.

And woke to sunlight, fragile and perfect, the dawn chorus in the woods.

There had been a bear. Called Ralph. Guzzling Coke in her kitchen. She laughed then, laughed at herself, and the absurdity of waking dreams, of chasing spirits and guides, rose up and let the throw drop back to the rocker, opened the screen door into the kitchen. And halted. There were empty cans all over the floor.

Did I do this?

Very likely. That could be the only rational explanation. She bent and gathered up the cans, tossed them in the recycling bin, checked the fridge and decided a trip into Lion's Head was what was required. A shower first. Then breakfast in the village, scoop up some groceries, and head back. She needed to get out more. Needed to get outside of her head. That was what was needed.

Later, when she stood in the checkout, watching supplies being deposited into her bags, Ellis, who was punching at the cash register, had just extended an invitation to come and have supper with her and Petra.

"Ralph will be there too," she said.

Ralph? Her heart kicked. She scratched the palm of her left hand, looked down at the red blotch there. A very bear-shaped blotch. "Ralph?"

Ellis laughed and nodded to the man standing in line behind her. Bearded. Mountain-man bearded. Sort of honey-brown bearded, dark eyes under winged eyebrows, and he whuffed a laugh.

"Ralph?" she said. Her mouth felt dry.

He winked. "Got under your skin already, I see."

She looked back down at her palm, up at him. "You?—"

"Pretty much. Hey, whoever said spirit guides were easy?"

Fall Arrest

Alice was sure her brain was going to leak out her ears, the pain was that bad; not ameliorated in the least by the stomping, panting, growling ministerial boxes taking up residence on her desk. *Why did I ever let my world enter Wonderland?*

"I really need something for this headache," she said.

Hatter, much-changed thanks to remedial counselling and skills upgrade training, poofed out of view and returned smelling of herbs and incantations with a bottle ominously labelled DRINK ME.

"You're not serious," she said, eyeing the bottle.

He looked at the bottle, back at her, blinking like an owl. "Oh! You don't think.... I mean you can't possibly imagine.... No, no it's simply an analgesic, like, like—"

"Like Aspirin?"

He nodded helpfully. "Some sort of pain medication, I'm thinking?

"You sure about this? I'm not going to shrink, or grow, or become covered in green spots or the like? Nothing of that sort?"

"Never heard of anyone doing anything of the sort from just plain old willow bark extract."

"The apothecary was—"

"A recognized and accredited one, yes."

He looked crestfallen, and she felt a git for questioning him like this. She gestured for him to hand over the bottle, unstopped it and tossed down the bitter contents as if she were doing shots, which she wished she were. By now the boxes were a cacophony of demands, some leaping up and down on top of other boxes, boxing, as it were.

"Stop it!" she snarled, and they halted. One teetered precariously on the edge—which reminded her of that bureaucratic and irrelevant fall arrest program she needed to be running with Humpty Dumpty, and all the King's Horses, and all the King's Men. Denizens' Workplace Compensation Board indeed. She made a grab for the box and was anticipated by dear Hatter who rescued the lovely cloisonné container. With a flourish, he returned it to her desk and admonished the box not to harry his Minister so, and to be patient, she would get to the boxes' contents in due time and in orderly fashion. They nudged and jostled and stilled under his glare.

Such a changed man, she thought, and smiled at him.

He pulled that plate of a pocket watch from his waistcoat, peered at it meaningfully. She groaned.

"I really don't want to do this," she said. "All those horses and stamping about. Humpty gormless as they come, bless his fragile self.

"We could always postpone the remedial course, you know," he said.

"That would be the third time, and we all know what happens when things run in threes."

"Another three." He shuddered. "Then let me deal with the boxes and at least send acknowledgements while you run the course."

"Dear Hatter," she said, touched his sleeve and left her office in Wonderland's Department of Denizen Resources.

When she reached Humpty Dumpty's wall, TweedleDee and TweedleDum were already there, harnesses and lines in hand. At the foot of the wall, the King's Horses and Men milled about, the horses themselves nickering and betting as to whether Humpty would succeed this time. Scuttlebutt had it—and she would have to query the Department of Gambling whether his betting license was valid—that Humpty would succeed, giving odds at 10:1. As she passed Scuttlebutt, she offered him her most incendiary look.

Humpty was sweating as she offered him a cheery hello. She didn't think that was a particularly good sign for an egg—to be sweating.

"We're going to take this nice and slow this time," she said to her team and Humpty. "Check things twice. Proceed with care and caution. Get Humpty that accreditation. Right?" They all nodded. Well, Humpty sort of grimaced, not having a neck or anything that would allow him to nod.

She could feel her headache easing, though she was still finding it difficult to focus on the task at hand. She felt a little light, sort of untethered.

While she supervised Humpty through the routine of harnessing up, tying off, one of the King's Men marched over, harrumphed, and then said, "Oy! Who's goin'ta be makin' up fer our loss o' work, then? Me and me mates wanna know, being as the Union o' Royal Workers 'as to be satisfied, like? Says 'ere clearly wots Kings' Horses an' Men must be present at all events in which Humpty Dumpty participates."

Her brain was leaking out her ears again, but not from pain this time. "You're here aren't you?"

"Well, yes, but—"

"And will be every time Humpty appears outside of his own, er, nest. That much doesn't change."

"Yeah, but there won't be no more pickin' up 'is pieces and tryin' to put 'em back together."

"That's a simple revision of job description, not a loss of job, a matter you'll have to take up later. Send me a box." To add to the others. She wondered what a box from their union would look like? Probably have a mane on it and leave steaming piles behind it.

Unless it were diapered. Could a box be diapered?

She giggled. What was she doing giggling? This fall arrest exercise was serious stuff. Ahem.

"Humpty, you need to tell me what you're doing," she said. "Tra-la, tra-lay, or—" What? "'Cause if you fail this time, it's going to be tulgey wood and vorpal blades for you." What am I saying?

She shook her head and gulped down bubbles of giggles. TweedleDee nudged TweedleDum, and said, "She's blotto."

I am not blotto! "I am not blotto!" She snapped her fingers at TweedleDee, and bladed her neck with her hand. The message was clear enough, and rather than have the entire Ministry of Denizen Resources down his neck, TweedleDee prudently practiced silence.

"You still need to be calling off your checks," she said to Humpty. He had by now managed to secure his body support harness and was looking for a suitable anchorage.

"I'm going to use a rope around one of the crenellations," he said.

Good choice! He hadn't thought of that before. Maybe there was hope.

Was he getting nearer, or was she closer to him? At least her head no longer hurt. It just felt detached.

"Anchor secure," he said.

"Good," she said.

"Connector secure," he said.

"Great," she said.

"And will now attempt to arrest the fall." At which point everyone was silent, and she was most definitely eyeball to egghead with Humpty, and watched him topple over the edge, the crenellation tear away, and shell, yolk and egg white splatter on the paving with a sound somewhere between a splosh and a crack.

And she was looking down at it all. Down. Not at. Not level. But from up here to down there, where Kings' Horses and Men, and TweedleDee and Dum, and Uncle Tom Cobbly and all were high-fiving and laughing, and joyfully shovelling up the pieces into a bucket where, despite all efforts, Humpty himself would pull himself together to once again face the hazards of The Wall.

What the hell was in that willow extract?

"Hatter!" she yelled. He popped into view at the top of the wall. She flailed in the air to bring herself about, trying very hard not to simply float away on her bubbling giggles. They were purple now, those giggles. She squinted at Hatter. "Wherever you got that potion, I want you to contract for more. Next time we run a Fall Arrest Program it's going to be with that apothecary's brew instead of harnesses." And then we can all get high together. She giggled again, and urped a sphere of pale lavender.

"Very good, Minister."

"And get me down from here."

"Very good, Minister."

Fall arrest program indeed. Just wait until she got her hands on those ministerial boxes back in her office! Then there would be some falling and arresting and tumtum trees battled into submission, or she wasn't Alice.

Occupational Hazards

OR

THE QUITE CURIOUS TALE OF ÁSTRIDR GRÍMSDÓTTIR

First published in Neo-opsis, Issue 25

The first time Ástridr spoke to him three things happened: he dropped his fine round number six brush into his cup of scotcher-tea; the scotch in the cup surged over the rim and crashed like a miniature tsunami onto the blue wash on the illustration; and the third was that his heart ricocheted around his chest.

"Lord Thunderin' Jesus," Ástridr said, when her artist didn't respond. In fact he just sat there clutching the neck of his sweatshirt. "Whadya go and give me a mouth like that for?"

"Um," her creator said.

"Well?"

"Um...."

"C'mon, c'mon, you think I want to have this thin, parsimonious mouth? Be a little generous if you're going to draw me. Give me a collagen mouth, you know, with them full plumped-up lips, Mick

Jagger-like, you know. Lips you could trip over." Ástridr blew a raspberry that seemed to indicate she might be able to fly if she had said prodigious lips.

Her creator – Eric Conner – meanwhile dabbed frantically at the spilled scotch-er-tea, considered wringing out the contents of the sponge into the cup, thought better of it and swished the sponge around in the water basin that sat beside the glass painting surface. With his other hand, he drained the contents of the cup while holding the brush firmly in place, grimaced, set cup with brush down, and then tried to repair the halo effect growing on the sheet of paper where his tea interrupted the drying of the wash. It was better, he decided, to ignore the gnome glaring at him from the illustration. Story illustrations didn't talk. They behaved themselves, politely if you please, and remained where they were drawn, keeping critical comments about physiognomy and most especially lips silently behind colour and ink.

"Oy! I'm talkin' to you!"

Eric made a noise he thought sounded like a whimper, and turned away to the desk drawer where he was sure he had emergency libations for his empty cup. But maybe that was the problem. It was only eight of the morning and he already drained two cups of tea. Well, one and a half. But still, the point was, even his granda would have disapproved of tea before noon. After that you could drink tea till you fell down snoring on the carpet. One needed to exercise a little decorum about these things.

And there was this deadline to consider. Damn all deadlines anyway. Reluctantly, he acknowledged time had a way of expanding into a deadline. Three months now shrank to tomorrow at noon. Noon, fergawdsakes.

He glanced back to the illustration that was to be the cover piece of a national SF magazine, a Canadian one at that. This was career making. Well, okay not career making, but certainly way up the ladder from his rung.

But there was that gnome. And damnhim if it weren't standing, hands on hips, glaring up at him.

"I'm not an IT," the gnome said. "I'm a SHE. And SHE wants better lips than this. Didn't you read that story you're supposed to be illustrating? Plainly not, else I wouldn't be yammering on about these pathetic lips you've given me. It says right there," she pointed in the general direction of his laptop, "paragraph three, line eight: *and with full and succulent lips, Ástridr said to her foe....* Full and succulent, it says." Ástridr pointed to her lips. "If this is your idea of full and succulent, then you need to read the dictionary. Oh right, you don't read. You just illustrate."

"I think I'm drunk," Eric said. He slumped into the chair. The back ratcheted down with a rasp and a bang. "Bugger."

"Here, give me that brush!"

Eric glanced over to the brush that still protruded from the now empty cup. He rescued it, stuck the sable end in his mouth, and sucked on it, savouring the last smoky dregs of scotch.

If he painted out the lips would the gnome stop talking?

"What you starin' at?" Ástridr said. "You need to start rectifying this botch of a job you've made of me."

No argument there. Maybe he should just erase the whole damned character; in fact just chuck the whole sheet of paper into the recycle bin.

Did the story really say Ástridr had full and succulent lips?

He swung round to the laptop and scrolled down to the passage Ástridr – was it really talking to him? – had indicated.

Yep, there it was: *and with full and succulent lips, Ástridr said to her foe....*

Damn!

Eric took the brush out of his mouth, waggled it in clean water and sloshed a pool of madder, sienna and aureolin together on the palette. That looked luscious enough.

"Hold still," he said to Ástridr who rampaged around the confines of two dimensions, muttering imprecations about shoddy masonry and thatch, and how her bodice should be red, not brown, and that shield should be round, instead of pointy. "You'll end up with a smear instead of puckering petals if you don't hold still."

Ástridr glared at him a moment, hanging upside down on the edge of the cottage's thatch roof, appeared to consider the proposal and decided to trust her creator to set things right. She stepped from eaves to wall to cobbled street as delicately as you please, struck her original pose and batted her eyes in what she plainly considered an inviting manner.

Eric touched the paper with the back of his hand, feeling only a dry response, which was good: otherwise the pigment on the loaded brush would bleed out over Ástridr's face, perhaps beyond, and there'd be more to worry about than full and luscious lips. In fact, there'd be full and luscious lips for gawdknew how far.

"Hold still," said Eric. And held the tip of the brush to Ástridr's mouth, scribing with fine, careful sweeps the suggestion of a kisser that would rival even Angelina Jolie.

"Tickles," said Ástridr.

"Better?" Eric asked."

Ástridr started to purse her lips when Eric shouted, "Don't!" Ástridr froze. "Move and you'll disturb the pigment. You don't want your mouth running, do you?"

Ástridr gestured with her hands to indicate she would hold her face perfectly still. In the meantime, Eric wheeled away from the work table and set about pouring together a cup of tea, no additives. Tea in hand, he scrolled to the top of the story the artistic director had sent him, and set to reading The Quite Curious Tale of Ástridr Grímsdóttir. Almost from the outset the story had Eric snickering, and by the time he reached the end of Ástridr's gnomish adventures, he wiped his eyes, catching his breath and exploding periodically into fits of giggles.

Damn that was good! Why hadn't he read the blasted story earlier? In fact, what had given him the idea he could just skim the adventure and get enough out of that to do a proper homage to the author's work?

He turned back to Ástridr who waited demurely on the page, lips gorgeously plump. With the back of his fingers he tested the dampness of the paper. "You can move now," he said.

Ástridr blew a kiss. "Thanks, eh?"

"You were right, of course. I should have read the whole story. Would have saved a lot of trouble."

"Well, it was only me lips."

"A little more than your lips. You're right. The thatch is shoddy and so is the masonry. Apparently you gnomes build things well. Among other things."

Ástridr flashed him a smile. "Now you're getting it, me boy. Saves other potential problems too."

"Oh?"

"How many writers have fired off incendiary letters of complaint to editors and artist both because their work has been misrepresented?"

Ah. "That too."

"And remember, no tea until afternoon."

Eric raised his cup to her. "No additives until afternoon."

"And then in moderation."

"Right." Eric set down the cup and picked up his round six and flat ten brushes. "Let's just get these last details washed in, let you dry a bit, ink what needs it, and get you scanned and sent off, shall we?"

"Sounds perfect. Say, maybe my author will write another tale about me, and you and I can work together again."

Eric laughed. "That's an occupational hazard I'd be willing to risk. Now hold still while I deepen the red of your hair...."

Trade Paperback 6 x 9, 372 pages $21.99
ISBN 9781988274614 eISBN 9781988274621

There is a conversation that should have happened between Vi Cotter and her mother. Now it's too late.

But sometimes the dead speak through the legacy they leave, and in this case Vi's mother bequeaths her, among other things, her journals. Do we sometimes seek absolution from the grave? Do we seek reconciliation between the child, the woman, the crone?

In a story of unspoken truths and hidden fears, The Rose Guardian explores the cages we make when we fail to unlock our secrets.

This is both a powerful and moving story that is told with sensitivity and heart. Masterfully crafted, this book is well worth reading. Highly recommended.

LibraryThing

Definitely recommend The Rose Guardian and look forward to seeing what else Ms. Stephens has written.

Goodreads

The Rose Guardian Preview

Endings

I realize now innocence, once lost, can never be retrieved. We yearn. We search. But that search is vain; only the vestiges of what we once had remains.

It was of innocence I thought as the officiant droned on. He spoke of a woman he didn't know. He attempted to convince those of us gathered in that sombre and neutrally appointed room Una Cotter was someone to be remembered, a vital part of her community, loving mother, devoted wife. There was no denying she was all that.

Una Cotter, descended from Norman conquerors. Or so she liked to say.

I remembered a woman I both loved and feared. There was little of softness about Ma. Estranged, widowed, hardened by experience, she was as capricious as Canadian weather. The only thing on which you could depend was in her winter, it was bitter. In her summer, it was glorious.

White Cotter roses bookended the funereal urn of plain, penny-wise stoneware; a digital display on the wall above, sequencing through images of Ma from femme fatale to fatal crone. She died so very small, coiling into herself as though gathering all her effort for one final, full-colour explosion.

I had few illusions I would escape the repercussions of that explosion, like thunder in the heart, or the tsunami after the quake. For now, there was this calm. I should feel something, I told myself. Surely this marked some sort of personal shortcoming that I couldn't squeeze out even one tear. As a woman of age, had I become as impenetrable as Ma?

Finally, a pause in that fabrication from the lectern, and in that space a song about time to say goodbye, meant I was sure to elicit profound weeping from the host of mourners. Ma was like that. I didn't know whether to laugh or rage, to feel fondness or scorn. How was I supposed to feel after all these years, after all this history?

I could hear someone cough, the rustle of cloth as bums shifted on padded seats, the breathing of so many people who had come to mark the death of this enigmatic woman. I stared at my knees where black silk noile draped down to touch the tops of my black leather flats. I wanted to shift my own bum, rid myself of the casing of spandex designed to make the Rubenesque feel svelte. Or at the least acceptable. Dear god I was getting too old for this.

I wondered vaguely if they'd stuffed Ma into spandex underneath her funerary garb. Or had they simply taken her to the crematorium and incinerated her, gardening clothes, gloves, and all?

My brother, Bennet, who in true Irish form styled himself Benneit, sat to my right. His wife and their adult children were behind us.

Ben glanced at me. He was as always clean-shaven, beautiful in a hoary, stag-like way, and closed as he had been since he learned we were not fully siblings. How long ago was that? Fifty years? Somehow the taint of that was something he'd never accepted. Or forgiven. As if I was responsible for our parents' shortcomings.

I wished I could read him, gauge what lay beneath that polished exterior, wished somehow we could regain the laughter and lunacy of childhood. I managed a smile, not much more than a lift of the corner of my mouth, an attempt to say I know, it's okay, death is just part of life. But Ben didn't need that. Ben, like Ma, knew how to survive. They were both expert masons. Their walls were impenetrable.

Ah, there was the great, fully-orchestrated crescendo I'll go with you upon ships across the seas, seas that exist no more....

I glanced to my left where Uncle Ianto sat, and good the gods he bent over his knees, tongue between teeth, a quarter clamped in thumb and forefinger. What was he doing?

"Uncle Ianto!" I hissed. "For the love of god!"

That song went on about being together, forever, endlessly on.

He looked up at me, an idiot grin on his face and a mesh of lines around those recklessly blue eyes. He turned his attention back to the task of deconstructing the kneeling rail in front of him. I should upbraid him, I thought, tell him to show a little more respect for his sister's memory. The officiant shot a frowning glance in my uncle's direction. I had the strangest urge to giggle. Jesus God, hold it together! If I started now I'd never stop. And then would come those tears I thought myself incapable of shedding. Foolishness. Liar.

No. No tears. I swallowed, wishing for this service to end, wishing for home and the sound of waves on the shore, of loons and their wild asylum cry.

I wanted to help Uncle Ianto take apart every last rail—Uncle Ianto who likely had more understanding than any of us about this funeral and what we marked.

Thank god, an end to that saccharine song.

The officiant—what was his name?—made one last futile attempt to urge either Ben or me to deliver a eulogy, and when met with a fidgeting, twitching silence, broken only by the scraping of Uncle Ianto's makeshift screwdriver, intoned his last words on the subject of Una Cotter and made his way to the door. That was a signal, I supposed, the service was at an end.

I elbowed Uncle Ianto to his feet, and managed to get him to leave off his deconstruction. We shuffled by the officiant, grasping hands, thanking him for his efforts. There was no invitation extended to him to join us at Ma's for the small refreshment we'd arranged. Mean spirited, I'm sure, but none of us needed this hired mourner to intrude upon the acrimony to come. That kind of vitriol is best savoured among the willing few.

We retired to the room set aside for family. Ben was already in discussion with the funeral director. I stepped forward to join in, thought better of it and retreated to where coffee had been provided. I swirled cream into a cup, watching it shift and billow, then finally settle into beige, heard my name and turned. Ben was there, introducing me to our host. What the woman said I hadn't a clue. It all seemed lost in a bubble. Nodding and smiling seemed in order, so I did that, shook her hand, mumbled thanks.

Ben took the velvet bag the woman handed him, hefting it to the cradle of his elbow. She withdrew. I looked over to Ben, tried to articulate my thoughts, but he said, "We're taking her ashes back home. I figured that was okay, given history."

He might have asked. I wanted to offer a bridge, found myself without the equipment to do so, and so only said: "Of course, Ben. Whatever you wish." But then, from somewhere, the courage to say: "I've missed you."

He seemed startled, his face softening for a moment. I saw the boy, my brother; then the man reasserted himself and Ben was lost to me. "We live in an age of communication."

I didn't think you'd want to hear from me—left unsaid, not knowing how. "I'm sorry," came out instead.

"So am I." He glanced down, then to the door. "We should go."

"Of course." Easier to fall back on duty. Easier to leave the demons chained.

Escape wasn't to be swift. There were the niceties of polite society, the acceptance of people's apologies–for what did they apologize?–the offer of comfort, of empathy, hands grasped and joggled meaningfully, faces full of well-intentioned emotion meant to convey solidarity in the face of the enemy of death. There were even hugs, unsolicited, unwelcomed, and my impotent hand patting a shoulder, a back, lips responding with platitudes and clichés, and the brain running ahead, anticipating bridges that might be blown or secure. Navigating. Always navigating.

"Should you need anything, Violet——"

Who was this? Don't remember. "Very kind of you to offer. We're all good. But thanks." The withdrawal of my hand from the clasp of two, a vague attempt to remember a name for that face. Glancing off to the doorway where Uncle Ianto fidgeted, laughing of all things.

"I need to get him in check," I said to Ben who stood next to me. "Rendezvous at Ma's." No response. None expected. I steered a course through the flow of bodies, keeping my attention anchored to my recalcitrant, unpredictable uncle.

At last I hooked my hand around his elbow, and head down, beat a retreat to the parking lot.

Relieved was how I felt when I buckled myself into the car, a moment's respite. I could feel Uncle Ianto about to explode into comment and criticism. What was it about the Cotters made us so willing to shake our fists, rattle sabres, beat shields? We should all just paint ourselves with woad and be done with it. Go charging off with the Wild Hunt.

I closed my eyes, feeling sunshine hot and penetrating on my face. A balm, a blessing. If there were any heroes in our family they'd long since vanished in the mists of Ireland, too insubstantial to make the journey to Canada. We were refugees, all of us, whether from famine or history made little difference.

"The hell with your brother," Uncle Ianto muttered. "Unmitigated shit!" I laughed, opened my eyes and turned to him. He looked like a radish. Blood pressure, I thought. Time to calm him down. "I never liked that little turd." That last salvo apparently just for good measure.

"Hush, Uncle Ianto," I said. "Let's just get through this." I raised a warning finger to him. "No shenanigans, okay? Behave yourself."

"Damn right, my girl. Damn right. Get through this and get back home."

I really am getting too old for all this melodrama, I thought.

It was about a twenty-minute drive from the funeral home to Ma's. On the way, Uncle Ianto and I spoke mostly about our plans for the remainder of the day and his departure tomorrow. It was agreed we'd try to quickly wrap the après deuil, have a quiet evening together, and stay in touch throughout the following week. I'd keep the car, drive Uncle Ianto and David— my ex—to the Waterloo airport where we'd arranged a hitch on a small charter. David would drive Ianto home at the other end, stay with him while I was away. David, another dangling thread in the fabric of my life.

But for now, we'd be a team, my uncle and I, with David conscripted in; we three dispossessed in uncertain territory.

I headed west out of Paris into the triangle of rural country between Highways 401 and 403; mostly flat, arable land now given over to the growing of ginseng and cereal crops, a few upstart vineyards creating nouveau vintage by marketing the ashtray flavour of tobacco to youthful trendsetters. Orchards joined those vineyards along with agritainment farms for the urban family seeking reconnection with the land.

When we turned north and rattled along the washboard gravel sideroad that led to Ma's farm, I felt my heart stutter. The last time I'd travelled this road I'd been in tears, David dispensing advice and indignation in equal measure at the wheel of the car.

Twenty-five years ago. And too many years of silence before we found a way through the fog of that particular war. It's always too late for regrets.

I slowed when I approached the maple-lined laneway, observed for a moment the old stone house, a Loyalist, utilitarian box, twenty-six windows, and one thousand acres of land given over to woodlot, a pond that was more a lake, and gardens that would have put any public horticultural centre to shame. The service entrance for the business side of Ma's property came in from the north, and it was there the trial beds of Ma's roses were situated, along with the greenhouses, labs, and office facilities. At least that's what I remembered.

Crown land deeded to the immigrant Loyalist Cotters.

"Still a sight to behold," Uncle Ianto said. "She always had style, did your Ma."

She did.

I eased the car up the shaded lane and drove into the courtyard created by virtue of a converted carriage house to one side of the house, and a renovated stable to the other. All, apparently, a reconstruction of the farm the Cotter's had left behind in Burt, Donegal. When I stepped out onto the gravel drive I paused, listening, remembering it was quieter when I grew up here. You had to go a long way north now before you could achieve that kind of quiet, where the reverberation of traffic didn't underscore everything. I had that at home, at my refuge at Meldrum Bay.

Then the mood was broken by a goldfinch's trilling, a sound to penetrate the heart and fear, a song of such joy as to make a mockery of the sombreness of a funeral. Here was life.

Are you there? Are you there? I still thought of goldfinches as throwing queries into the air.

I looked to the copse of trees in the distance, trying to find the brazen yellowness of the bird. But no. Only that glorious sound, and despite myself I smiled, allowing such simple pleasure to touch my apprehension.

I scanned the lawns, the gardens, watching a little girl dart amid the rose parterre, her red capris and white shirt as defiant as the goldfinch's song.

"Who's that?" I said, nudging Uncle Ianto.

He looked up at me, frowning. "Who?"

"That girl."

"Where?"

"There." I nodded to the parterre where this imp of a child now stood, waggling an admonishment at a white rose.

"Yer daft," Ianto said. "There's no girl there. Just Una's roses."

I opened my mouth to protest, snapped it shut. She'd gone. No matter. I steered Uncle Ianto past other vehicles in the drive, guests who plainly arrived ahead of us, along to the front door that was thrown open to the beauty of this May day. Ma would have fetched a fit. Letting in mosquitoes and blackflies and who knew what vermin. Nature was perfectly fine kept ordered and in its place, all ugliness eradicated.

My nephew, Colm, greeted us in the foyer, all hugs and exuberance, tall and no longer the boy I remembered. He laughed with Uncle Ianto, found someone to guide our fey relation into the parlour and get him settled and seated. Alone with Colm, I asked, "Would it be silly of me to say you've grown?"

He grinned and looked down at me. "A bit, Aunt Vi. But I'll forgive you." He gestured to a diminutive woman beside him. "This is Aislinn." I shook her hand, raised an eyebrow to Colm, who said, "We've been together a few years now."

"I'm the last to know anything." I nodded into the house. "I gather your father doesn't approve?"

"Living in sin and all that."

"We just didn't see the point in contractual love," Aislinn said. "And weren't sure how you'd feel, so we just kept things quiet."

I smiled. "Manitoulin's a long way away, but you're always welcome. You and Colm both. Might as well find out how the rest of the non-conformist Cotters live."

"It's a date then," Colm said. "Give me your keys and I'll fetch in your bags." Colm gestured to the parlour off the foyer. "Dad's in there with Mum and Erin. I know for sure at least the females will be glad to see you."

"Thanks for the warning."

I stepped through the wide archway into the parlour, dodging ghosts and memories, listening to the susurration of voices both present and past. Not much had changed since last I was here. Light still flooded the room from a long bank of deep-set windows. There the fireplace with its ornate fire-screen and potted plants, the Regency-style sofas like bookends, the butternut bookcases and leaded glass, leather volumes carefully arranged alphabetically by author. The Heppleworth knock-off secretary, the Persian carpets, occasional chairs in conversation groups for conversations that never took place.

"Can I offer you refreshment?" my sister-in-law was asking, I realized. I turned toward her.

"It's good to see you, Evelyn." I declined the offer of a drink. "The only time we Cotters seem to gather is at weddings and funerals, and not so much the former as the latter." You're being unfair, I thought.

"It was a lovely service, don't you think?" she said.

"Mmm, yes. Ma had it all arranged, I'm sure."

"Down to the obituary notices for the papers," Ben said, drawing abreast. He watched me over the rim of his glass, garnet wine catching the light. Why was it I always felt there was subtext?

You're too paranoid. Just fergawdsakes stop being so damned anti-social.

I gestured to a settee and eased to the jacquard cushions, fitting myself into a corner. A shrink would rub her hands with glee over that, I'm sure. Uncle Ianto, radar zeroing in on potential family conflict, thumped down in the opposite corner of the settee, looking like a cornered hound.

There was an uncomfortable pause, and then my niece arrived, all effervescence like her brother, and asked about life on the island. I responded, asked about her doctoral studies.

"Bio-ethics isn't it?" I said.

She confirmed, talked about the Third World crisis in medical care, of human experimentation by the giant pharmaceutical companies, and while I watched her face illuminate with passion, I thought I couldn't be too harsh on Ben and Evelyn if they could create a woman with this kind of commitment and intelligence.

It wasn't long before her brother joined in the debate, and that kept us all occupied for the next twenty minutes. By now other guests arrived. The room filled, people spilling out onto the back terrace where spring breathed. Where I needed to breathe, so I rose from the sofa, made my excuses, and wove my way through mourners to the freedom outside.

A surprise, yes. Ma's death was quite sudden.

In good health? Yes, she had been in good health. Or so we thought.

Stroke. Yes. A surprise. Yes, a surprise.

I wondered what it had been like for her, ass to the heavens in the garden, endlessly eradicating weeds. Had there been pain, a dizzying moment of disorientation? Had she pitched into her beloved roses and wondered if now, these many years and sins later, she was to meet her Maker. Had there been fear? Had there been regret? Had she been lonely, dying alone, the perfume of flowers her last absolution and sacrament?

I found myself sitting on one of the stone benches in the rose parterre, remembering when first Ma had taken spade and shovel to the ground, digging out the shapes to make a Maltese cross and medallion. I had been no more than five or six. She had been frenetic, I remembered, furious, tears cascading with sweat down her face, her dark hair a jumble of curls escaped from the bun in which she customarily contained it.

I had wanted to comfort her. But even that young I knew Ma's view of comfort was grim, a sign of weakness.

"You're not to come home from school with your father," she'd announced suddenly. "I've made other arrangements."

I didn't ask the obvious, the genesis of a lifetime of avoiding crisis. Dad hadn't been at dinner that night. Nor at breakfast the following morning. Nor any meal thereafter. Our neighbour became my after-school ferry and safe house while Ma earned our keep. Uncle Ianto came to live with us about a year later, after Ma had been in hospital.

"They talk to you if you listen."

Startled, I looked to my side, unaware I'd been joined by the little girl I'd seen earlier. She shifted her bum on the cool stone of the bench. I smiled.

"Who talks to you?" I asked.

"The roses."

Such a serious little face. There wasn't any artifice there, not even a suggestion of mischief.

"The roses talk to you?"

"Sure. Don't they talk to you?"

They used to, I remembered, after Ma planted them, encouraging slips she'd nurtured in the greenhouse, a feather forever in her pocket with which she'd dust and broadcast pollen like a human bee.

"Not for a long time," I answered.

She considered that for a moment, then: "Well, maybe they're just waiting for you to say something."

"Vi!"

Startled, I looked up, bringing into focus a face I knew well. I swallowed regret. "David. You came. I was just talking to—" I looked to where my young guest had been to find only the cold bench.

"Yourself?" David asked.

"No. To…where did she go?"

"Who, Vi?"

"The little girl I was talking to."

"There's no one here. Just you and me."

"But…I…." I winced, looked back up at him. "I'm glad you came," I said instead, confused, suddenly unsure of everything and this entire day.

"I promised you."

"That was gracious of you. You certainly didn't owe Ma anything."

He shrugged. "I owed her at least for the gift of knowing you."

I looked down and away. "I suppose the whole bloody island knows."

I heard him laugh, looked up at that familiar face. "It's a big island." And together we said, "Largest fresh water island in the world," and giggled like kids caught telling a dirty joke. He joined me on the bench.

"You sure you're okay taking care of Uncle Ianto?" I asked.

He nodded. "It's all set. We'll get back to Gore Bay tomorrow afternoon, late. Just came down for the service and to help with Ianto. I'm staying at Featherstone's B&B tonight if you need me. You figured about two weeks you'd be here?"

"About that. There are apparently details of the will that need to be addressed fairly soon for the smooth continuation of the greenhouses and guesthouse. Not sure how long that will take. I'm hoping we can get the majority of it addressed in the next two weeks while you holiday with Uncle Ianto, and then I'll take care of any further details via email and the like."

"Good thing the ferry's open. It'll make getting back easier for you." He nodded toward the open doors of the terrace. "You and Ben talked?"

"Not really. Hasn't been time yet."

"You going to be okay?"

I laughed and ran my fingers through the cropped curls on my head. "Oh sure. You know me."

"Tough old bird. Like your mom." I stiffened, looked at him. "Vi, relax. All I meant was you're a survivor, whether you realize it or not. All of you Cotters are. It's just that in you, survival doesn't come at someone else's expense." I closed my eyes on tears, sudden and hot, felt the rough tips of his fingers along my jaw. "If it weren't for her…."

"I know," I said, looking at him, at that face I'd known and would always love. "It was an unfair war in which I placed you." I kissed the tips of his fingers, pushed his hand to his chest where I let mine linger a moment. "I should go mingle." Stood and left.

The room and Ma's mourners enclosed me. In the end I sank back into the corner of the settee where I'd started, sipping water. Conversation flowed and ebbed around me. I answered questions, offered comments and gratitude, pulled a smile from my pocket of theatrics and pasted it on my face. I wished there was booze in the cup, was grateful there wasn't. After awhile the afternoon became a blur and then past tense as the door closed on the last guest, and Ben brought us back to the funeral, and the miracle of medicine that had allowed Ma such longevity.

"Ninety-four," he said.

"Ninety-eight," I said, and once again realized how much she'd risked, even then. She'd always said it hadn't been convenient for her to have children. Convenient. Children. Yes, that was Ma.

There was an uncomfortable pause, and then I said, "I suppose we should talk about the logistics of the estate. I can spend a few weeks down here to help. It's not like my boss is going to fire me."

"That's true," Ben said. "Unlike you, some of us do have responsibilities to employers."

I closed my eyes, chewing on the bait, rejecting it. It was just Ben's way of stirring things up. "I have a show coming up, but I'm well ahead," I said.

"Where are you showing?" Evelyn asked, arriving with a new tray of refreshments and fixings. There was a moment's interruption as people moved to clear space on the coffee table.

It was Uncle Ianto, ever my defender, who answered, "She's showing at the Manitoulin Festival of Art."

"Ah, art for the indigenous," Ben said.

"It's a fundraiser," I finished, throwing Uncle Ianto a warning glance. What I didn't want was an all-out fracas. Bad enough we fired ranging shots each other.

"I can do this on my own," Ben said. "There's really no need. But thanks."

"Really, it's okay," I answered. "I figured I could go over the will with you tomorrow, start organizing. I thought it might take some pressure from you." And now he knew where I stood. I wasn't going to be sidelined, and while it wasn't like I was hoping for some buried treasure to be unearthed in this sorting of the deceased's effects, I did want a chance to be alone with Ma's memory, with the possessions she'd gathered around her like a shield. Nope, Ben didn't like that one bit. What I wasn't prepared for was his next statement.

"The will's been changed, you know."

Ah, there it was, the quake. "Oh?"

He smiled. "You and Uncle Ianto are welcome to read it."

"You've got that right, my boy," Uncle Ianto said. "Isn't that so, Violet, my flower?"

"Perhaps we can do this tomorrow morning?" I asked. And suddenly I felt as though my navigation had foundered my ship. Why couldn't anything to do with Ma ever just follow a simple course?

Ben swirled the wine in his never-empty glass. "Actually, there's a meeting over at the greenhouses with the CEO of Cotter Greenhouses tomorrow morning to discuss the smooth transition of the greenhouses and business. But of course, if you'd rather not attend...."

I hesitated a moment, never good in the line of fire.

"I can go with you," Uncle Ianto said.

Not a great idea. "You're travelling home with David."

"But—"

"I saw him here. David." Ben said. "I thought that was all washed up?"

"People are capable of civil separations, you know."

Ben snorted. "Ah, my sister the diplomat. You'll talk yourself into anonymity."

"And have a clear conscience."

He shrugged in that judgemental way he had. How was it he could raise violence in my sensibilities where no one else could? All I wanted to do was break my fist on his face.

It was Colm who said, "Whoa, Dad. Ease up, eh?"

I threw Uncle Ianto a look I hoped would convince him of my need to be here alone for the meeting.

"You sure?" he said.

"Absolutely." I turned back to Ben. "It would appear it's settled."

"Suit yourself," Ben said. "Nine. Ma's office. You remember?" He didn't wait for an answer. "I've retained some of the hired staff for the next few days."

"I don't know why," Evelyn said. "It's not like there's going to be an army of guests."

"My wife isn't serving my employees."

My employees. Ah. Then the will made Ben the new major shareholder of Cotter Greenhouses. As much as that information stung, I wasn't surprised, which was in itself a surprise. First the quake, now the tsunami, the stutter in the heart. I couldn't even bring myself to wonder why, once again, Ma chose to overlook me. Was I incompetent? Was that it? Was the fact I'd run away from her and a marriage and confrontation enough to tattoo failure on my forehead? How was it I could be a senior citizen and still feel like six even in the memory of her presence?

"Right then." I set my cup on the coffee table and rose, turned to Evelyn who looked bewildered by the duel that had just taken place. I managed a smile. "It was lovely, as always, to see you, Evelyn." To the kids: "If you're going to be around, would love a chance to chat over the next few days, catch up a bit." I levered Uncle Ianto to his feet. "C'mon, you. Enough excitement for one day." And made my way to the stairs, Uncle Ianto ready to sputter. The moment I had him in his room he broke into an uproar. And through it all he muttered, "The little shit."

I let him rant. Sometimes it's good for the soul to scream at the gods. Just be careful they're not listening. There was enough momentum in his anger it carried him through my administration of his meds, which usually was enough of a chore, and overseeing his trip to the loo.

"You can manage your pyjamas?" I asked.

"Of course."

I wagged my finger at him. "Don't you of course me. I know you. If I don't do a bed check you'll be sleeping starkers in the chair or flashing at the window."

"Oh, now, Violet, that's hardly fair."

I retreated to the door, continued to wag my finger at him.

"Behave yourself. Pyjamas and right into bed. Your book's on the nightstand."

He thumped down on the edge of the bed and glared at me. "You're no fun when you're serious."

"And you're a pain in the ass when your balls are in an uproar."

"Such language."

"Go to bed, Uncle. And behave yourself."

He clucked a disgusted sound and waved me away. I closed the door on him and made my way to the adjacent bedroom where memories would ooze from familiar furnishings.

Despite my assurances to Uncle Ianto, I was under no illusion the settling of Ma's property would be smooth.

I ducked into the bathroom while the rest of the family were downstairs, removed cosmetics I detested, brushed and flossed, and padded my way back down and across the hall to the room that had been mine in another life. When I closed the door, I felt I might drown. There wasn't enough air. It was too congested with memory in here, and all of it bittersweet, both joy and sorrow, laughter and anger. I eased to the edge of the bed, remembering a satin-edged blanket where there was now a down duvet, flounces of floral bed skirts where now a neutral box-pleated skirt hung stiff with starch. But the bedframe was the same, cherry posts and headboard, a blanket rack in the footboard where one of Ma's amazing quilts hung. She had a way of painting with fabric, of employing colour and texture.

I slathered moisturizer onto my face, feeling the push and shove of my skin, no longer supple, ever thirsty, let my fingers linger over my closed eyelids, paused, swept in and up, paused again, and this time knew there were tears and that despite all my denial, all my own carefully built mechanisms, grief eroded it all.

Unable to face myself in the light, I snapped off the switch on the lamp, leaned over and curled myself onto the bed. I watched the last vestiges of the day darken from crimson to indigo behind the maples.

Why was it I always seemed to be crying myself to sleep in this bed?

I woke with a start in the night, heart skittering, disoriented, a face from childhood like a ghost in my mind. This wasn't home. This wasn't my bed. I could hear voices, and for a moment I thought perhaps there were trespassers on my property. With a jolt I sat up and realized I was in Ma's home, that she was dead, and we presumed upon her hospitality in her absence.

I eased off the bed, crossed to the armchair by the window and sank into it, after a moment opening the sash to the cool night air. It touched my face as I sat there, a relief, scented with wisteria and grass, the verdure of the garden. Far off there was the tenor whirr of an eastern screech owl, mysterious and lonely, and beneath that the spring treble of peepers and toads.

My heart stilled. It had been thumping, silent to all but me, the way an owl's wings beat unheard by both prey and predator. In that suspended moment, I wondered if I fell, like an owl from her perch, would I be able to effortlessly push away the air once, twice, rise in disdain of gravity and glide across the meadow to that far line of maples and spruce, find the gnarled ancient that spread limbs over the spring that fed the lake, and rest. And watch the water that flowed ceaselessly, deceptively warm to invited skin even in the bitterest of winters. Would I see that face again? Would those fingers rise as liquid cascades like skin shedding? Would I be able to conquer my fear? This time? Would I?

I let out a breath, gathered another, slowing my frantic thoughts, gathering reality and order out of the shreds of dreams and old fears. It had been decades since I'd thought of that face, a child's ripe imagining in the blue-green waters of a sulphur spring.

I looked up and out the window, feeling the night air bathe my febrile cheeks.

There was a full moon caught in the arms of the willow I called Grandmother as a kid. It always reminded me of her, of Grandma's long hair that she'd let down and allow me to brush in those rare, still evenings. When she was gone, and all that was left was her book of Shakespeare's sonnets and a lingering impression of the dowager empress, I began to sojourn with the willow, seeking out Grandma's spirit beneath its graceful cascade, reciting poetry she'd encouraged me to memorize. Ma did not approve. I was never sure if it was because of her impatience with my romantic adolescence, or the fact I broke curfew by escaping into the willow's variegated moonlight.

It seemed to me I was always part of her disdain quotient. Certainly, it was her disdain that finally shattered my fear of her and led to me not only hanging up on a telephone conversation with her, but smashing the phone into plastic gravel.

It was an outburst of violence that had shocked David, I remembered. He'd enfolded my rage into the harbour of his arms, while I gasped out my wish for her death. Careful what you wish for.

We were married two days later. Only Uncle Ianto and David's sister attended the civil ceremony. And from there we'd migrated north to Manitoulin and the hope of a life free from Ma's influence.

But sometimes we allow a person to linger in our minds, permanent residents that shadow all our brightest moments.

Chiaroscuro. That was Ma.

And since then not a word. Either of us could have easily picked up the pieces of that conversation, glued together some semblance of a working relationship, mended pride. Yet I found myself incapable of forgiving her for her condemnation of David and our marriage. What were her reasons for silence I would now never know.

All that was left was regret.

I leaned back in the chair and apparently allowed the moonlight and cool night air to lull me finally into sleep. I kept hearing that wee girl's voice: They talk to you if you listen.

If you listen.

It was my niece, Erin, who woke me with coffee and a smile.

I sat up in the chair, full of imperative.

"It's okay, Aunt Vi," she said. "You have an hour."

"Uncle Ianto—"

"Is up, dressed and downstairs breakfasting thanks to Colm. We thought we'd give you a break. It's going to be hard enough for you getting through this meeting with Dad and the team at Cotter Enterprises."

"Thanks," I muttered, and took the cup into my hands, sipping this forbidden, rich brew. "You two staging a mutiny?"

"Oh, Colm and I have pretty much always teamed up with Mum to keep Dad in check. You Cotters, you know."

Erin squeezed my shoulder and retreated. I took a few moments to let the coffee work its magic, and then set about making myself presentable. A meeting with the executive of Cotter Enterprises was something for which I'd been unprepared, and rummaging through my suitcase after showering I realized I'd have to cobble together an outfit from the jacket and shirt I'd worn yesterday with the only pair of dress pants I'd brought with me. Jeans and t-shirts wouldn't cut it, and there was no way in hell I was going to struggle into spandex and pantyhose, let alone bother with cosmetics.

With a despairing glance at my wet and unruly head of curls, now mostly grey, I headed downstairs. I could hear David as I descended the stairs, the rise and fall of his husky voice. Down the hall I could see Uncle Ianto's suitcase by the front door. I turned right into the dining room where I found David, sitting back in one of the chairs, his legs stretched out and crossed in front of him, completely at ease as was his wont. Colm looked up from across the table, grinned. I murmured a general greeting, waved off offers of breakfast from the small buffet on the sideboard.

"Car's picking us up in half an hour," Ben said.

"We couldn't walk?"

"You can. You'd better get started. It's a hike."

"Take the car," Evelyn said. "Leave the walk for when you're not on a schedule."

"Good point," said Colm.

"The indignities of getting older," I said, which generated a few chuckles and a stony silence from Ben. I wanted to confront him, ask exactly what it was I'd done wrong, why he continued this antagonism. After all this time I just wanted a little peace. But the truth of it was I was afraid to open the subject, afraid of what might result. Learned responses have a way of creating negative instincts.

The moment passed when David sat forward and nudged Uncle

Ianto.

"We'd best make tracks," he said.

"You're carting me off, then, is it?"

"Afraid so. We've a flight and then a bit of a drive."

As a unit we all rose and followed David and my uncle to the front foyer, embraced, and said our farewells. Colm and Aislinn stood with them, a ferry to the charter.

Uncle Ianto patted my hand. "It will be fine. Never you mind."

I looked at the gnarled knobs of his knuckles, hands that had known hard work. "You think so, do you?" I said.

He leaned close and hugged me, whispered in my ear, "Shall I come with you, take apart the chairs just in case?"

I laughed, pecked his cheek, and turned him toward the door. Watching him drive away I smiled again thinking of him bent to the task of deconstructing rails. The memory seemed almost inappropriate given what was to come, and even more so when Ben announced what we all could see, that the car from the office had pulled into the courtyard. He descended the steps without another word to either his children, his wife, or me. I supposed that could be considered adversarial.

It was later I understood there was nothing adversarial in Ben's actions. His was the surety of the victor.

About the Author

Lorina Stephens has worked all sides of the publishing desk: writer, editor, publisher. From freelance journalist for regional and national periodicals, to editor of a regional lifestyle magazine and then her own publishing house, she's been at this professionally since 1980 and witnessed publishing evolve into the dynamic form of self-expression which exists today. For 12 years Lorina operated Five Rivers Publishing as a house which gave voice to Canadian authors. Due to life circumstances, she had to change direction, and so now the house exists as a bit of a vanity press for her.

Lorina's short fiction has appeared in literary and genre publications, novels under Five Rivers Publishing, non-fiction under Boston Mills Press and an anthology co-edited with Susan MacGregor, *Tesseracts 22: Alchemy and Artifacts*.

Mostly she's an introvert. You won't find her at conventions. On social media mostly Lorina lurks. If you really want to know what she's about, read her work. It's that simple. If you're curious, email her at: lorina@fiveriverspublishing.com

Other Books by Lorina Stephens

And the Angels Sang, trade paperback and ebook

Caliban, trade paperback and ebook

From Mountains of Ice, trade paperback, ebook, and audiobook

Memories, Mother and a Christmas Addiction, trade paperback and ebook

The Rose Guardian, trade paperback and ebook

Shadow Song, trade paperback, ebook, and audiobook

Stonehouse Cooks, trade paperback and ebook

AVAILABLE THROUGH FIVERIVERSPUBLISHING.COM
AND YOUR FAVOURITE ONLINE BOOKSELLER